"Do You...
Of Coffee?"

Megan asked nervously.

"What I want is *you*. If I come in, Megan, I won't leave until morning. Is that what you want?" Luke framed her face with his hands. "I want to taste you. Your lips have been driving me crazy since the first time I saw you. I want to know if they're as soft as they look."

Megan's gasp of surprise was a sharp sound in the still night air. "I told you that first day I wasn't interested," she whispered.

"You lied."

"Luke, this will only complicate matters."

His grin flashed in the darkness. "All I want is one kiss. You can stop me. All you have to do is say no, but I think you're as curious as I am. As hungry as I am..."

Dear Reader:

Welcome to Silhouette Desire — provocative, compelling, contemporary love stories written by and for today's woman. These are stories to treasure.

Each and every Silhouette Desire is a wonderful romance in which the emotional and the sensual go hand in hand. When you open a Desire, you enter a whole new world — a world that has, naturally, a perfect hero just waiting to whisk you away! A Silhouette Desire can be light-hearted or serious, but it will always be satisfying.

We hope you enjoy this Desire today — and will go on to enjoy many more.

Please write to us:

Jane Nicholls
Silhouette Books
PO Box 236
Thornton Road
Croydon
Surrey
CR9 3RU

Hot Property
RITA RAINVILLE

*First published in Great Britain in 1995
by Silhouette Books, Eton House, 18-24 Paradise Road,
Richmond, Surrey TW9 1SR*

© Rita Rainville 1994

*Silhouette, Silhouette Desire and Colophon are
Trade Marks of Harlequin Enterprises B.V.*

ISBN 0 373 59399 6

22-9501

Made and printed in Great Britain

RITA RAINVILLE

has been a favourite with romance readers since the publication of her first book in 1984. Rita has always been in love with books—especially romances. In fact, because reading has always been such an important part of her life, she has become a literacy volunteer and now teaches reading to those who have yet to discover the pleasure of a good book.

Other Silhouette Books by Rita Rainville

Silhouette Desire

A Touch of Class
Paid in Full
High Spirits
Tumbleweed and Gibraltar

Silhouette Christmas Stories 1992
"Lights Out!"

To Paul, Virginia and Adam Rainville with love—
you know how special you are

Prologue

Hawaii, June 29, 1890

She said yes.

Before the year's end, my sweet Jenny will be my wife.

Inarticulate as I always am when my deepest emotions are involved, I almost bungled the whole thing. With any other woman I would have. But Jenny knew. She knew that behind my frozen, pompous words I was telling her I loved her, that I would protect her and cherish her for the rest of our days.

She deserves so much more, to hear words of love and promises for a lifetime. Someday she will. Someday the words will surely come easier to me.

In the meantime, I will build her a home, one with my love poured into the very foundation, nailed into every board from the floor to the rafters.

When she steps through the front door, she will understand. Yes, my Jenny will understand. Just as she did this evening.

When she said yes.

The lean man slowly closed the journal, absently stroking the leather binding with a large hand, wishing it was Jenny's silky skin beneath his fingertips.

Jenny. With her love-drenched eyes and deep feminine courage. She could have the pick of any man on the island and she had chosen him. *Him.*

He got up and locked the book in a metal chest, protecting it from the humidity. As he slowly turned the key, his dark eyes narrowed with determination.

She would never regret choosing him.

She would *never* regret it.

One

"No, it's not what you think, Mr. McCall. I'm a healer, not a hooker."

Ignoring his startled blink, Megan Murphy eyed the tall man lounging in her doorway. His chin was square, his dark eyes assessing, and he exuded disapproval. She gave a resigned sigh. "At least, that's what my family tells me. The bit about healing, I mean. Not hooking. It's these." She held up her hands for his inspection, waggling slim, tanned fingers. "They're supposed to have a healing touch."

"And do they?" The question was as skeptical as it was reluctant.

She shrugged, refusing to be charmed by the unexpectedly deep voice. "Darned if I know. Frankly, my family's a bit on the dramatic side and I think they simply enjoy the mystique—as well as having someone around who can give them a damn good massage."

He frowned. "You're a masseuse?"

She slowly shook her head. "Not really. I only do it in my spare time for family and friends, and I'm not certified. I just have a knack for it. And that's what I've been doing for the last ninety minutes, Mr. McCall, working the kinks out of my cousins—who, by the way, just finished a grueling soccer game—not having my wicked way with a clutch of young men. Now, would you like to come in, or do you want to stand in the doorway blocking the light while you tell me why you're here?"

She turned around, heading for the lanai, wondering if he believed her. Probably not, she decided with another sigh. He had had plenty of time to draw some conclusions while he prowled the perimeters of her yard, waiting, and she had a sneaking suspicion that those conclusions hadn't been flattering. No, Lucas McCall didn't look like the type who automatically gave one the benefit of a doubt.

She also wondered if he would follow her, then wondered if she really wanted him to. Having grown up with four brothers, their friends and a multitude of male cousins, she was normally comfortable around men, but this one already had her on edge. He looked hard, determined and more than a bit stubborn, the kind of man who knew what he wanted, went after it and usually got it.

Normally she appreciated those qualities because she shared most of them, but not today, not right now. Something in Lucas McCall's dark eyes told her that what he wanted just might be her. At any other time, the prospect might be intriguing, but today what *she* wanted was a job, not an affair. Leading him anywhere was flirting with danger, a bit like inviting a hungry tiger to a picnic, she reflected, trying to ignore the tingling at her nape. If he came, she just might end up as lunch.

Luke followed her inside the restored plantation house, torn between watching the tantalizing sway of her hips and inspecting the welcoming room.

The hips won.

They—along with the rest of her gentle curves—were wrapped in a swathe of blue fabric held together by sheer willpower or some mysterious bit of feminine magic.

Walking behind her, he silently admitted that Megan Murphy wasn't what he had expected to find. When she had been unanimously recommended for the job of restoring the three plantation houses he had recently purchased on the Big Island for bed and breakfasts, he'd assumed she was older. She had a reputation for bringing old places alive, for maintaining the integrity and simple beauty of the original structures while subtly integrating all of the desired modern conveniences.

She was practically a damned legend. Everyone in the industry seemed to know her or of her reputation. If you want the best, he had been told, she's it. She was as independent as Madame Pele herself, but good. So he had opted to bypass the telephone and go take a look at a living legend.

What he hadn't expected was a long-legged beauty with auburn hair and deep blue eyes. But that was exactly what he had found two hours earlier, when he'd impulsively driven to her house to offer her a job. Hell, to *beg* her to take the job, if she was flexible enough to incorporate several of his ideas into her work.

Driving the short distance from his hotel to her house had only taken a few minutes, small potatoes compared to some of the trips he'd made in the past looking for local talent. He wouldn't have hesitated to go farther. Since he made a habit of getting the best—and she seemed to be it—Megan Murphy was who he wanted.

Apparently she was also good at other things, he had decided a few minutes later as he'd watched a handful of men milling like restless stallions in her front yard. It hadn't taken long to discover the attraction. She had appeared in the open doorway, wearing a smile and a sarong, a single, fiery braid draped over one shoulder, almost reaching her waist.

Before his mind had even registered her full impact, Luke had sucked in a breath, feeling his body clench. He'd wanted to smooth that sensuous coil of hair with his fingertips, to touch the cinnamon wisps that brushed her forehead, following the curve of her brows. To slowly unwind the strip of material wrapped around her. Actually, he'd wanted to do a hell of a lot more than that.

But what he had done was watch her gaze drift over the men and smile at their restless prowling, watch as she singled one out, crooked a commanding finger and said, "You." Watch as she had ushered the lucky one through the door and followed him inside. Watch as twenty minutes later she had repeated the routine with another man.

When the last one had disappeared and he had knocked at the door, she had taken one look at him and seemed to know exactly what he was thinking. And now, following her through the gracious old house, he thought about what she had said, tried to believe the men were cousins, that she had merely been massaging sore muscles.

It wasn't easy.

"Things are never easy, are they, Mr. McCall?" Megan asked softly, startling him again. "And quite often, they're not at all what they appear to be."

Ignoring the question, Luke asked one of his own. "How do you know who I am?"

Megan took her time answering. First she led him through the living and dining rooms and out a side door to the lanai.

Waving him to a green wicker chair with bright cushions that was shaded from the May sunshine, she said, "I read the business section of the newspaper. You've been in it a lot lately."

She sat in the matching chair across from him, waiting while he examined the oval swimming pool and the pink roses peeking through the white rails enclosing the veranda. His gaze drifted over the painted wicker furniture and the glass-topped tables and ferns. She leaned back, giving him all the time he wanted, knowing he liked what he saw.

She would show him the rest when he was ready. It was, after all, obviously the reason he had come. It was the only reason that made sense, in spite of the speculative gleam in his dark eyes when he glanced her way. And since the two-story house was her pride and joy, her home as well as her office and business showcase, and she wanted him as a client, she would give him the fifty-cent tour.

Megan contemplated Lucas McCall's profile. It definitely wasn't the kind found on Greek coins, she reflected. It was strong, extremely masculine and without a trace of elegance. Thick hair, heavy peaked brows and lashes the color of freshly brewed coffee were the only softening elements. No, this one hadn't been born with a silver spoon in his mouth, she decided. Somewhere in the not too distant past, the impressive Mr. McCall had a number of street-brawling relatives.

He had undoubtedly refined the trait a bit, but he hadn't come up the ladder the easy way. Even if she hadn't read about him, it would have been easy to deduce that sheer guts and hard work were the primary elements of his success.

His eyes were as dark as his hair—brown or black, or a bit of both. His nose had started out straight, but somewhere along the way it had encountered a fist or some other hard object. Now there was an intriguing ridge dead center. His lips were well-defined, neither too narrow nor full, and they were flat-out sexy. And his chin? Polite people would call it determined. They would be wrong; it was obstinate.

The rest of him was just as impressive. Or intimidating, depending upon one's point of view, she thought wryly. He stood a couple of inches over six feet, lean and well mus-cled. He wore his casual slacks and shirt with the same air of cool competence that characterized all of his actions. Apparently, he put them on, told them to behave, and they did. Without wrinkling. In the present humidity, that was no mean feat.

His hands were surprising. Large, with long supple fin-gers and strong wrists, they were not the hands of a rich man who sat behind a desk all day. The backs were sprinkled with crisp dark hair and the palms were callused. They were the hands of a man accustomed to hard, physical work.

And all that was just on the surface, she thought, shift-ing restlessly. It was what was hidden beneath that was re-ally making her nervous. She had decided she was being whimsical when the image of a tiger presented itself, but now she was pretty sure it had been right on the mark. Lucas McCall looked every bit as sleek and dangerous as a large cat.

All told, he was a daunting prospect. Rich, accustomed to being in charge and too sexy for his own good. Or hers. A wise woman would think twice before getting involved with him—in business or pleasure.

Megan sighed, acknowledging an unfortunate fact of life—although the Murphys were known for many things, self-preservation wasn't one of their outstanding character-istics.

"I was going to call you," she said abruptly when his dark gaze shifted back to her. "When I read that you bought the three plantations, I decided to make an appointment with you to discuss the restorations. I want the job.''

Luke's brows rose. Annoyed at the relief pouring through him, he said contrarily, ''Just like that?''

Megan shrugged. ''You obviously know who I am, and you just cut through the preliminaries by showing up on my doorstep. You're interested, and you're here. So am I, Mr. McCall.''

''Luke, Megan.''

She tilted her head, examining his face. He was probably hell on wheels in a poker game, she reflected, because it didn't give a clue to his thoughts. ''Just like that?'' she asked, giving him back his own words. ''Luke and Megan? No introductions, no questions?''

''You're the one who said we skipped the introductory song and dance. But I do have a question.''

''Just one?''

''For now.''

She waited, then, before he could ask, she stood and said with a touch of impatience, ''No, I wouldn't have shown up for an interview in this.'' She smoothed a hand down the clinging material. ''I would have worn something business-like. One of my sedate, show-'em-what-a-hotshot-you-are suits.''

Remaining where he was, Luke stared at her. He didn't blink or move a muscle. The expression in his eyes could have been fascination, revulsion or any point in between. Megan couldn't tell. She had been on the receiving end of glances like that since childhood—whenever her quick tongue betrayed her flashes of knowledge—and they weren't any easier to deal with now than they had been then. When he suddenly smiled, she found it equally confounding.

''Then I lucked out, didn't I? I'm glad I got to see you on your own turf, barefoot and touchable.'' He surged to his

feet in a smooth move that blended such lazy strength and
sheer masculine grace it left her blinking. "And that's the
third time you've done that," he said levelly.

"Done what?"

"Read my mind."

"A handy parlor trick," she said lightly, refusing to get
sidetracked. Especially on that subject. "It runs in my
family. Now, do you want to see the rest of the house before we talk business?" When he nodded, she turned, leading him to the dining room. He came to a halt beside her,
standing so close she could feel the heat from his big body.
Tension feathered her nerves, tightening her stomach muscles, and she carefully edged a few inches away.

Luke gave the room a swift, encompassing glance, taking in the textured, stucco walls and the golden, rattan furniture. Overhead a silent fan looped in slow circles, sending
drifts of cool air toward a lacquered cabinet and a table that
would easily seat twelve. Books, native artifacts and bas-
kets of green plants rubbed shoulders, giving the room the
warmth and grace of an earlier time.

"I like what you've done in here," he said quietly.

She didn't try to hide her pleasure. "Good. If you like
this, you'll love the rest of the place. Come on."

Less than an hour later, back on the lanai, Megan handed
him a glass of iced tea and looked at him expectantly.
"Well?" She leaned back, trying to read his expressionless
face. As usual, he wasn't giving much away. But he had
liked the house. Loved it, as a matter of fact. Which was just
as it should be, Megan thought complacently. She was good
and she knew it. Now he knew it too.

"How far are you willing to go to get this job?"

Megan stared at him, her nerves jangling. He couldn't
have actually said that, she told herself, trying hard to be
convinced. In this day and age, no man with a modicum of

business savvy would ask such a blunt, outrageous question. He might think it, but he wouldn't ask. If his own common sense didn't muzzle him, the thought of a woman confronting him with accusations of sexual harassment certainly would.

When he just sat there, waiting, she realized he had. Damn it, the man actually had said it! "*Mis*ter McCall," she began, spitting out the words like icy pellets, "I—"

"Luke," he said calmly.

"Whatever. I think we need to get something straight. I want this job, but I don't *need* it. Do you note the distinction here? I was excited when I read about your plans for the old places because I had some ideas along those lines myself and—"

"You wanted the properties?"

She shook her head, saying tersely, "No. I didn't want to buy them. I wanted to restore them. But as much as I want the job, I don't play bedroom games to get work."

"Neither do I."

"Sure. Then what was that nasty little question all about?"

"Nasty? What the hell are you talking about?" He blinked, obviously trying to recall his exact words. Megan knew the second he did. Anger blazed in his dark eyes. "You thought I—?" He swore, succinctly and colorfully. "Look, lady, when I make a move on you, you won't have to wonder. You'll know. There won't be a bit of doubt in your mind."

"Forget it, Mr. McCall. I'm not interested."

"I am," he said flatly. "And you will be. But we won't do anything about it until after we settle our business. And speaking of business, if I had said that to a man, he would have known exactly what I was talking about."

"Terrific. But, since I'm obviously *not* one, why don't you translate for me?"

"Time," he said succinctly. "And effort. And management. I know you have other jobs, and I need to know if you can reschedule things, how fast you're willing to hustle so you can get right to work on the first house."

"Oh." Megan knew she sounded as disconcerted as she felt. Hiding her feelings wasn't one of her major accomplishments.

"Yeah, *'oh.'*" He waited, watching her expressive face, then said, "Do you think you can swing it?"

"Yes."

His brows rose. "You don't want to think about it, look at your calendar?"

"I'll sort it out." Even if she had to work twenty hours a day. "We haven't talked about money," she reminded him. "You don't have the foggiest idea what I charge."

"Money is the last thing we'll argue about," he assured her.

"Oh?" She tilted her head thoughtfully. "But you do think we'll argue?"

His eyes gleamed with sudden amusement. And promise. "Inevitably. I'm looking forward to it. But, right now, my main concern is that we have a mutual..."

"Vision?" she suggested when he hesitated.

He nodded. "Exactly. I've got some ideas I'd like to show you. Wait here while I get them out of the car."

Megan followed him, stopping on the wide front porch and leaning against the rail while he strode to his silver BMW and grabbed a briefcase. She wondered idly if he actually expected her to copy another designer's work, if he had any idea how offensive the idea was. She knew the answers immediately: yes, he did and no, he didn't.

He truly didn't understand that, in her own way, she was
an artist, she reminded herself as he turned toward her.
Perhaps not the caliber of Monet or Rembrandt, but an
artist nonetheless. It was as simple as that. And like any
good artist, she measured her success by the quality of her
work. Money was nice, but since wealthy clients often came
hand in hand with abominable taste, she selected her jobs
carefully. Ultimately, it was her decision, her judgment. Her
work. Hers.

And now she didn't need ESP to suspect they were heading for trouble. In their first—and probably final—major
disagreement, they were about to butt heads, ideas, philos-
ophies and visions. But since he didn't understand, she
would be kind. And patient.

Then minutes later she knew she'd been right.

The slim file he had given her contained drawings of
rooms, supposedly in a plantation house. The sketches were
slick and professional. They were also boring, predictable,
relying heavily on ferns and wooden masks. Even worse, a
fleur-de-lis, the McCall hotel signature, was tucked into the
wallpaper in every room.

"Who did these?" she asked in a noncommittal voice.

"A designer who worked on my last hotel in San Francisco. I liked some of his ideas but not enough to give him
the job, so I paid him for the work and kept the sketches."

Megan winced, knowing that what he liked was the
blasted flower on the wall. "San Francisco?"

"Yeah." Luke took the file from her and slid it back into
his briefcase. "You don't like them?"

"Let's put it this way," she said, striving for tact. "It's not
the kind of thing I do."

"You wouldn't incorporate some of these ideas into your
plans?"

Sure. Over the dead bodies of both herself and her twin, Devin. Megan looked at Luke, her thoughtful gaze resting on his chin. Obstinate, she reminded herself. "Maybe now is the time to discuss our vision," she finally said. "Exactly what is it you have in mind for the bed and breakfasts—Hawaiian kitsch or authenticity?"

She was already kissing the job goodbye, he thought grimly, keeping his gaze on her expressive face. She was doing a miserable job of hiding her frustration. "I want it to look like a comfortable old plantation house. I want it warm and welcoming. I also want people to know it's part of the McCall chain."

"And do you want them all to look alike? If that's the case, you don't need me—especially since you have your own ideas. Any decorator on the island can help you. If it's authenticity, however, then we need to talk about how I work."

"I'm listening."

He wasn't a happy camper, she reflected, but he got points—a lot of them—for hearing her out. She held up a slim finger. "First of all, I never repeat myself. My hallmark—if I have one—is originality based on authenticity. And charm. I bring out the best of the past and blend in the present." Another finger joined the first. "Second, I never use anyone else's layouts." A third finger rose. "I do all of my own research, come up with my own plans."

"You don't like these?" he asked again, tapping the briefcase.

Megan shrugged, knowing that she was about to toss away the most exciting job to come down the pike in a long time. It hurt, but she would deal with that later. "About as much as I'd like anything done by someone on the mainland who has probably never even been to Hawaii."

"I think some of his ideas are good," Luke said.

"You're entitled."

"You won't use them?"

Megan sighed. "Why did you come to me, Mr. McCall?"

"Because you're the best," he said promptly.

"Then why not let me do the job as I believe it should be done?"

"Because I'll be paying your salary, and that gives me a few rights. You're very stubborn, you know," he said mildly.

Megan nodded. "Yes, I am. And just as uncompromising when it comes to my work." Be kind, Megan reminded herself. And patient. "Do you like my house, Mr. McCall?"

"Luke." His quiet voice gave her the impression that he'd keep saying it until she finally did. "You know I do."

"I could give you one just as impressive."

"But without using the fleur-de-lis?"

Megan sighed again. "Probably not."

Megan held up a fourth finger. "My last rule. I don't haggle—over money or concepts. But I usually manage to produce some drawings before I alienate my clients. I'm sorry we didn't at least get that far." She set her glass of tea on the table and stood. "It was nice meeting you, Mr. McCall, but I don't see any reason to take up more of your time."

"Luke," he reminded her, again mildly. He took out a business card and scrawled something on the back. "Here's my hotel and room number if you change your mind. And, Megan, I hope you do."

She led the way back to the front door, managing not to mutter, "Don't hold your breath." She hesitated when he held out his hand. She didn't want to touch him, did...not...want...to...touch...him. In fact, she had

purposefully avoided any contact with him during his visit.
She knew by now that if she could get into his mind as easily as she had, even brushing against him would result in a
physical jolt.

But slowly, reluctantly, Megan held out her hand. When
he took it in his, it was as bad as she'd expected it to be.

Worse.

Heat and awareness swept through her like a rampaging
tide and instinctively she jerked back, putting her hand behind her in a protective gesture.

"If I don't see you again, good luck with your project,
Mr. McCall," she said hastily.

"We'll meet again." The gleam in his narrowed eyes re-
inforced the promise. Or warning. "And you might as well
get used to it. My name is Luke."

Megan watched as he walked down the path and slid behind the wheel of his car. He's just an ordinary man, she
assured herself as he drove away, refusing to think about the
rush of sensation she'd felt when he touched her. If they did
meet again, she could handle him. She was still trying to
convince herself when the telephone rang.

She reached for the receiver and said absently, "Hi, little
brother."

"Someday we're going to figure out how to do this without using the phone," Devin said. "And what do you mean,
'little'? A minute and a half is all the edge you have."

She could hear the smile in his voice. He had a point, too,
she admitted to herself. By no stretch of the imagination was
he little. He was every bit as tall as Lucas McCall and
matched him muscle for muscle.

"What's up, Sis?" Devin asked softly. "Who's bothering you?"

Not *what* she noted, but *who*. She was too accustomed to
their rare form of communication to be surprised. "Oh, I

just had an interview with a prospective client and it didn't pan out. It was...annoying."

"From where I'm sitting, I'd say he was a bit more than that. *Provoking, exciting* and *arousing* are a few words that come to mind. Sounds like just the kind of man you need in your life."

"Devin! For heaven's sake! It was a *business* meeting."

"Did you touch him?"

"Yes..."

"And?"

"I got a real jolt," she admitted.

"So, what did you learn about him?"

"You know, sometimes I really hate this stuff!"

"Come on, Sis, give."

"He wants me," she said, exasperated.

"I can't imagine why. That brassy hair and those weird blue eyes should have scared him away."

She smiled, just as he wanted her to. Devin was her spitting image—a masculine one, to be sure—cursed or blessed, however one saw it, with the same hair and eyes.

"So what else?"

She sighed. He wouldn't give up until he'd wormed everything out of her, until she felt better. "A big part of him doesn't want to want me."

"Doesn't believe in psychics, ESP and all that jazz huh?"

"I doubt it. He's more the type who only believes what he can touch and feel. But that's not it. He doesn't even know about my...peculiar gift."

"Oboy. What else?"

"He needs me. Part of him knows it and he's fighting tooth and nail, because he's about the most self-contained man I've ever seen. But it's also that he needs something in me. Maybe my warmth. My...laughter. Who knows?"

"Your liquid sunshine, Sis." His voice grew tender. "We all need it. Is there more?"

"Yeah. It sounds silly, but I feel ... bound to him. Don't ask me how, because I don't understand it myself."

"And?"

"I don't expect to see him again. We don't seem to agree about much. But if I do, and he needs me, I don't think I'll be able to walk away from him. Not *him* exactly, but his ... need."

Devin's sigh was louder than hers had been. "Maybe I ought to do a little checking up. Luke McCall, isn't it?"

She didn't bother asking how he knew. She knew only too well. "Devin," she said in alarm, "I want you to stay out of this. You *and* your detective agency—"

"Investigative services."

"Whatever. It doesn't belong in my personal life."

"Aha. You admit it's personal, not just business."

"Maybe, Sherlock. Maybe. Right now, it's a moot question because Mr. McCall and I have agreed to disagree. We probably won't see each other again."

"Baloney. What's the problem?"

"Ah, there *is* something you don't know."

"And you know why. Because unless we're with each other, we pick up each other's emotions, not thoughts." He waited.

"It's the three plantations he bought," she said abruptly. "He wants them restored. He even wants me to do them. The problem is he doesn't want me to do them *my* way."

"Is that all? Come on, Sis. Think. You can talk a man out of his right arm if you put your mind to it. Get a little creative here. And a lot less stubborn. If you don't, he might decide to turn them into glitzy hotels."

"Thanks," she said dryly. "That's just what I needed to hear." She fiddled with he telephone cord, knowing he was waiting, would wait for as long as it took. "Dev?"

"Yeah?"

"I think I'm afraid."

"Of him?" His voice hardened.

"Not that way," she said hurriedly. "He wouldn't hurt me. At least, not intentionally."

"Then what's the problem?"

"I don't know."

Luke stood at the penthouse window looking down at the aquamarine water. It reminded him of Megan's eyes. That shouldn't surprise him, he thought with irritation. Everything he saw reminded him of her. And he knew why.

He wanted Megan Murphy. Even if he thought she was as stubborn as an Arkansas mule. Even if she walked into his mind as if it were an open door. Even if his hand still tingled where she had touched him. Even if he remembered the ways she couldn't wait to kick him out of her house.

He wanted the humor lurking in those unbelievable blue eyes. And the intelligence. He wanted her in his arms, her fiery hair sliding all over him. He wanted her, period.

He stood there without moving, just thinking. There was a way. There always was. And he would find it.

Because, one way or another, he would have Megan Murphy.

Two

She wouldn't let him get to her.

Not this time.

Megan pushed the elevator button for the top floor and thought about the coming interview. She would be cool, professional. She'd done this too often to be nervous about it. It would be simple, straightforward. After all, brain surgery wasn't the issue here, it was just a job. There was absolutely no reason to be nervous.

She was overdressed, she brooded.

She could have worn slacks, a dress—anything but the prim forest-green suit. But she always made the supreme sacrifice of climbing into panty hose and a suit for a first meeting, and as far as she was concerned, this *was* their first business conference.

Tightening her fingers around the grip of the slim briefcase, she wondered if she should have left it behind. No, besides being necessary, it informed even the dimmest wit that this was a business call. Not that Lucas McCall was dim. On the contrary. But after the fiasco four days earlier, she wanted to be certain that he would have no doubts about this meeting.

She wasn't nervous, she told herself as the elevator came to a halt. She was saying it again, trying to convince herself, when the doors silently slid open, framing the green-and-gold penthouse foyer.

The fact that she had neither seen nor heard from Lucas McCall in four days simply meant that he was better at standoffs than she was, she reflected wryly. He'd been pleasant when she called, hadn't he? Of course he had. He had listened and calmly invited her over. He hadn't even gloated.

Yet.

"Is that one of your hotshot suits?"

Startled by the deep voice, Megan lifted her gaze from the button she was pressing to keep the doors open while she dithered. Damn. She was definitely overdressed. Lucas, wearing a white knit shirt, faded jeans and running shoes, was lounging in the doorway of his apartment, waiting.

For her.

His shoulder was braced against the jamb, his arms crossed on his chest. His inspection of her was leisurely and . . . nerve-racking. His dark gaze slid over her in open approval, giving her the shaky feeling of being smoothed by his large hands, stroked by callused fingertips.

Shivering, Megan stepped out of the elevator, narrowing the space between them. "The suit's all part of the image," she assured him.

"I'm impressed." A swift grin lightened his dark face. "I bet you knock them dead in the boardroom."

Expecting him to move back, she stepped closer. "Indeed I do, Mr. McCall. Indeed I—"

Lucas stretched out his arm to block the rest of the doorway. "The suit's nice," he granted, "but I prefer the blue sarong. And the name," he said evenly, "is Luke."

Megan waited, wondering if he was always going to keep her off balance. More than likely, she decided. At least, he'd try. He was a man who liked to be in control. Like right now. He wasn't going to move until he got his way. Until she said his name loud and clear.

She flipped a mental coin and decided that her knee-jerk reaction to him had already ruined one encounter between them. If she blew this one, there just might not be a third. And she wanted this job.

"Luke," she acknowledged with a sigh.

Dropping his hand and stepping back, Lucas waved her into the room.

He had converted most of the large room into a work area. On one side a long table bristled with electronic equipment—a computer, modem, printer and fax. Another was littered with architectural drawings and papers roughly stacked in piles. A sofa and a couple of chairs were clustered on the other side. There was nothing personal in the room at all. She realized that she wasn't surprised by the fact. Lucas McCall struck her as the kind of man who kept his private life just that. Very private.

Once they were both seated on the sofa, Luke said blandly, "I thought you didn't haggle."

She took a moment to settle her briefcase in her lap before looking up, knowing what she would see. She was right. Behind his bland gaze was the patient curiosity of a cat regarding a tasty mouse. His confidence was just as distracting, she reflected, not knowing whether to be amused or annoyed.

But there was nothing funny about the situation, she decided abruptly, because on a deeper level, awareness thrummed between them, distracting and full of tension. The potential boss wanted to know how she reacted under stress, but the man was sending another, completely different, message. And he would be very annoyed if he knew just how clearly she was receiving it.

"Has anyone ever told you how really annoying you are?" she asked calmly, meeting his gaze head-on.

He grinned and leaned back, draping a long arm across the back of the couch. "Nope."

"It figures. Well, Luke, I come from a family of resilient women and mule-stubborn men. I don't intimidate worth a damn. And what I'm doing isn't haggling." She gave him an exasperated glance. "I'm doing what I would have done four days ago, if I'd had any warning. I'm showing you some drawings, explaining a few ideas."

"And if I don't like them?"

"Why wouldn't you? You liked everything about my house, didn't you?" Megan allowed the exasperation to color her voice as she opened the briefcase. "However, if you don't, at least I've given it my best shot, rather than no shot at all. And should that happen, we simply agree to disagree."

She gave him a quick sideways look to see if he was still with her. "If I tried to change your mind at that point, *then* we would be haggling. But since I don't do that, I'd just go back to the work I already have, and you would look for someone else. However—" she pulled out several drawings and selected one "—I don't think that's going to happen."

She gazed at the sketch before turning to him. "I've given a lot of thought to your logo. It's elegant and distinctive, and it works beautifully in your West Coast hotels. But if you're aiming for authenticity over here, especially if you're dipping into the past, you need to have something..."

"Different?"

She narrowed her eyes. "Just modified so it's appropriate to the time period." Sliding the first drawing to him, she said, "Maybe like this."

Her nerves stretched to the snapping point as he studied the prototype of a magnificent Hawaiian male, dressed in a breechcloth, cape and headress, holding aloft a blazing torch. The flames of the torch rose in sinuous coils, gradually entwining themselves into the shape of a fleur-de-lis.

"This is authentic?" Luke shifted his gaze from the drawing to her expressionless face. One second was all it took to know that she wasn't as cool as she pretended to be. Her anxious eyes gave her away. He hoped the living legend didn't make a habit of bluffing.

"Of course it is," Megan said indignantly. When his brows rose, she added more slowly, "As far as it goes."

"What does that mean?"

She sighed. "It means that while I won't haggle, I *will* compromise. On certain things. Mainly on the aspects of marketing. This is a drawing of a high chief, one of the *alii*—royalty. One hundred per cent authentic.

"But the natives didn't own the plantations, and that's where the compromise comes in. This—" she indicated the drawing "—is what tourists visualize when they think of old Hawaii. It could be used as a sign in front of the house. The torch would be your island logo, for all your B and B's. It could be impressed in bars of soap, put on shampoo boxes, napkins—whatever you want, as long as it isn't part of the decor itself."

The corner of his mouth turned up in a quick grin. "So we keep the house clear of vulgar commercialism?"

"Absolutely. At least, if I do it."

Luke watched the emotions fighting in her blue eyes—hope, yearning and sheer, gutsy determination. The living legend might lose a battle every now and then, but she wouldn't go down without a hell of a fight. "What about the other drawings?" he asked noncommitally.

She handed them to him, saying frankly, "They're variations of the same theme. I don't like them as well as I do that one."

He looked at them quickly and handed them back, keeping the first one. "I don't, either. What about the house? Don't you have any sketches?"

Her direct gaze suddenly shifted to a point somewhere over his shoulder. "I, uh, prefer to do those on site. After I do some research." She tapped the corner of the drawing resting on his thigh, carefully avoiding contact with him. "This is step one. If it interests you, let me go out to the plantation and do some preliminary sketches. If you like them, I get the job. If you don't, you find someone else, but you can keep this. A present. Free and clear. No obligation."

"Okay." Luke nodded in abrupt relief. He had spent most of the last few days trying to figure out how to reopen negotiations between them and still keep a balance of control. Walking away from her hadn't been one of his smarter moves, but going back with his hat in his hand wouldn't have worked. Not with someone as stubborn as Megan.

He'd considered several ideas, rejecting them out of hand. None touched the heart of the problem—that neither of them would give an inch. He had finally decided to out-stubborn and out-wait her. Exactly thirteen minutes of his self-imposed time limit had been left when she had called.

He stood up and held out his hand to her. "When do you want to go? I'm free tomorrow."

Megan gave him a disconcerted look. "You don't have to come with me," she said hastily.

"No problem. I want to see the place again, anyway. I have to check out a few things."

She ignored his extended hand, busying herself with putting away her drawings. "Why don't you go tomorrow by yourself? That way, I won't bother you or keep you waiting. I can get the key from the realtor in a couple of days and spend as much time as I need out there."

Luke gave her a bland smile. "If tomorrow's too soon, I'll wait."

"No!" Megan blinked. When she looked up, his hand was still there. "I mean, you don't have to do that. I, uh, have a tendency to get lost in my work," she said earnestly. "I take a long time, and you probably have appointments. People to see. Things like that." Her words dwindled away. His alert expression told her she was wasting her time. What was worse, she could feel his curiosity, the flare of interest growing stronger with every word she uttered.

"Day after tomorrow will be fine," she said in a resigned voice, tentatively touching her fingers to his. One handshake to settle this part of the deal, she promised herself. That was all it would be.

"Good, I'll pick you up at nine."

Seconds later Megan was in the elevator, punching the button and watching with relief as the doors shut, enclosing her in a cocoon of safety. Damn it! There was no such thing as a brief, businesslike handshake with the man.

Touching him was like brushing against a live wire, and all it did was reinforce what she already knew. He wanted her. And with the single-minded intensity of a striking predator, he was determined to have her.

He wanted her.

It was that simple. There was no sentiment involved, no Romeo-and-Juliet forever-after involved here. It was pure, basic masculine hunger.

Sex.

And the idea of getting that close to him scared the hell out of her.

Megan took a deep cleansing breath. Touching Lucas McCall was almost like walking into his mind. It was a fleeting, involuntary trip on her part, one fraught with land mines. It told her much about him.

Too much.

Responsibility was a deeply ingrained trait. But at some time in his life he had closed himself off from the softer emotions, even though he took care of those smaller and more vulnerable. He did it because he believed he should, not necessarily because he wanted to. And she had a strong hunch that his feelings about women were just as controlled—that he thought in terms of mutual attraction and satisfaction. When both were gone, so was he.

That was a lot for a born romantic to deal with, Megan reflected wryly. He was a scary proposition for someone who thought in terms of love, commitment and making love.

And that was precisely why four days had passed before she had called him. Her reaction to him was too strong, too soon. He wasn't the kind of man she needed in her life. She might want him, but she was smart enough to stay away from a self-contained man like Luke. He could cut her up in slivers of grief. She wasn't a masochist, for heaven's sake. There was enough pain in the world without going out and looking for it.

A slight morning breeze was stirring the lacy leaves of the jacaranda trees when Luke pulled into the long driveway. Megan looked up and briefly stopped sweeping the lavender-blue flowers that coated the walk.

''Be right there,'' she called.

Luke nodded and leaned back with a slight smile. The legend was all woman this morning. A very enticing woman, despite the green walking shorts that met at a prim point between thigh and knee and the loose matching tank top. She could wear a blanket and still stop traffic, he reflected idly, watching the fabric tighten across her shapely bottom when she bent over to scoop up the flowers and toss them into a box.

Her fiery hair was bound again in a thick, long braid that touched the small of her back. A fringe of bangs brushed her forehead. The braid was like everything else about her—pure temptation.

He wanted to unravel it, let the silky mass spill through his fingers, coil around his wrists until—

"Sorry." Megan slid in beside him, tucking a straw bag neatly at her feet. "I love those trees, but there's a price to pay for the beauty. A constant clean-up job." She patted the dashboard of the black four by four. "Where'd you get this little baby?"

"Rented it." He backed down the drive and turned away from town. "The roads were a mess the last time I went out there. Sure you have everything?" he asked, glancing down at her tote bag.

Megan's gaze followed his and she nodded slowly. "I don't need a lot when I'm doing preliminary sketches."

"How do you normally research a project like this?"

She looked at him, puzzled. "I'm not sure I know what you mean."

Luke shrugged. "Projects where the original plans aren't on file anywhere. Where you have almost nothing to go on."

Megan stared straight ahead, watching the lush border of trees flash by. Don't ask, she thought. You don't want to know. "I have an old book of plantations at home that was compiled years ago by a local historian. My grandfather gave it to me when he saw where my interest in old places was taking me.''

That much was true.

It was immaterial that Luke's three acquisitions weren't in it. Nor were any of the other homes she had done in the last few years.

Success in her chosen field had convinced her that clients were more interested in results than methods. If she gave them the beauty and grace of an earlier time, they never even thought to ask where or how she got her ideas.

Until now.

She shot an aggrieved glance at Luke's profile. This one, she thought with a sinking feeling, was going to be different. Whether it was idle curiosity or something more instinctive, she had a hunch that he wasn't going to let the subject drop.

She was still brooding when the truck turned down a rutted dirt road. Lush flowering bushes formed a ragged bower of green around them.

"Road needs grading," Luke muttered. "And the bushes cut back," he added as several straggly branches slapped against the windshield.

"Don't let anyone come in and do a chop job on them," Megan said. "These are dwarf poincianas. They bloom most of the year and make a lovely entry to the property. Oh, my God, will you look at that," she whispered in awe as Luke rounded a bend and headed straight for the old house.

"What?"

"That. The banyan." She pointed to a huge tree with a massive root system. Leafy branches grew in all directions, creating a shady area larger than a tennis court. As soon as Luke stopped the car, she grabbed her straw bag and slid out, heading for the tree. When he caught up with her, she was leaning against the massive trunk, her eyes dreamy.

"Don't even think about cutting this down," she said flatly, not bothering to soften the direct order. "If you do, I'll come back and haunt you. People used to. . ."

"Used to what?"

She opened her eyes at the soft question and blinked up at him. "I mean, it's a perfect place for family gatherings and parties," she said hastily. "Can't you see lawn furniture with puffy cushions? And a swing, a glider, right—" she moved to stand a few feet away "—here."

"Can I get it trimmed?"

"Of course," Megan said absently, pulling a small leather pad from her bag and jotting a note. "It's badly overgrown and needs care. Everything does." She snapped the notebook closed and looked up at him, a rueful smile curving her lips. "Oh, you were kidding, weren't you? I'm sorry, I didn't mean to sound—"

"I think you did," he interrupted, stopping her before she perjured herself.

"You're right. I meant every word, but someday I'll learn to be more tactful. Luke, do you know what you have here?" Excitement deepened the blue of her eyes. "An absolute showplace! The yard is like an arboretum. Look over there."

She grabbed his hand and tugged until he followed her out from under the canopy of leaves. "That's a rainbow shower tree, and over there is a silver oak. And a royal poinciana. And that one, the one that looks like a big green umbrella, is a monkeypod. Oh, Luke, people are going to fall in love with this place before they even see the house."

Luke swore softly as he took in the tangled growth. His romantic historian saw the possibilities, but he saw the reality. "It's going to take an army to keep the grounds looking decent."

"I know just the man to handle it. That is, if you don't mind a personal recommendation. Mr. Kimura's an artist, and he's too ethical to charge what he's worth. He can turn this place into an Eden."

Luke nodded. "I'll give him a call." He took another assessing look at the large trees she had named. Beyond them were another dozen or so, all different varieties. "I don't see any order to the planting," he said. "It looks like the original owners just went out and dug a hole when they decided they wanted another tree."

"Oh, no." Megan shook her head. "These—" she stood in front of him and gestured to the large trees around them "—were planted for visual beauty from the front of the house. Those behind the house, spaced in a fairly large semicircle, were by the cottages."

Luke stiffened. "What cottages?"

Remaining where she was, with her back to Luke, she said innocently, "Didn't the realtor tell you that plantation houses often had cabins for the overseer and other important employees? That was the case more often than not."

"I didn't see any signs of them when I checked the property."

Megan shrugged. "No reason why you should. You weren't expecting them or looking for them, but I'll bet you dinner tonight that we find the foundations by the trees."

Luke curved his hand around her shoulder and squeezed lightly. "Dinner's yours. I don't bet on sure things. You name the place and I'll pick you up." Letting her go, he said briskly, "We've both got things to do. How do you want to work it?"

"Give me a couple of hours in the house. Alone. Please," she added, obviously as an afterthought.

Luke's brows rose. "Why the need for privacy? You do a voodoo routine while you're in there?"

Megan picked up her straw bag and scowled at him. "Very funny. I . . . just work better without distractions. Okay?"

"Okay," he said with a shrug, "but be careful. There are some weak spots in the flooring." He might as well have been talking to the wind. She was on her way, already absorbed in a time slot somewhere between the past and the future.

Ordinarily Luke would have had no trouble keeping busy for two hours. Today was different because he had nothing to do. He was there for one reason only—to be with Megan. Although his scheming hadn't done him a hell of a lot of good, he reflected wryly, watching her disappear into the house.

But it was a start. It wouldn't take too long to figure out what her startled looks and hesitations were all about. She was simply too open to be covering up dark secrets. Her expressive face would give her away in a second. As far as that went, it already had, several times. The problem was, he didn't know what it was revealing.

But he would. Soon.

That settled, he strolled over to the trees behind the house, looking for foundations. He found them beneath the brush and rampant growth, just where she had said they would be.

Interesting.

Maybe it was as common as she said. And maybe it wasn't, a skeptical little voice in his head whispered. He stood motionless, wondering, one booted foot resting on an exposed block of concrete. Megan was the local expert. As such, she could be trusted to get the historical facts right. But something felt wrong. He didn't know what, but he had learned by now to pay attention when things didn't feel right.

With still thirty minutes to go, and wanting to know just exactly how a living legend researched a site, he returned to the house. Quietly closing the door behind him, he stood in the living room, listening.

There wasn't a sound in the house. Whatever she did, he thought absently, she did it in absolute silence. Moving soundlessly through the rooms, he came to an abrupt halt in the kitchen doorway.

Megan was sitting tailor-fashion in the middle of the floor with her eyes closed, facing him, and she wouldn't have heard him if he had been a tank crashing through the walls. Her empty hands rested on her knees, palms up. No pencil, he noted. No sketch pad. Just a look of utter concentration.

Remaining as motionless as she was, Luke silently released the breath he had been holding. He had always considered himself a pragmatic man, a logical man, but right now, with his hair lifting on the back of his neck, he put all preconceived notions aside. Because he knew with absolute certainty that wherever she was, Megan was not in this room. At least, not in this time.

As if the startling thought had reached her, Megan's eyes snapped open. Without blinking, she met his dark, stunned gaze.

"Oboy," she breathed.

Three

When the doorbell rang that evening, Megan glanced at her watch and swore. Seven. Right on the button. She might have known that on top of everything else Luke would be prompt.

Earlier—when he had discovered her sitting on the kitchen floor—she had asked for a few hours' reprieve. Surprisingly enough, he had agreed. Probably so he could mull over the policy for firing a loony woman before she was actually hired.

But the bargain had been struck for more than time. It had included total silence. No questions, no conversation, just a ride home and time to herself. Again, unexpectedly, he had agreed. Beyond a few speculative glances, he had left her alone.

Now she had to pay the piper.

"I thought we were on for dinner," he said quietly when she opened the door. His gaze took in the shorts and tank top she had worn earlier, as well as the fatigue in her blue eyes.

"We are." She stepped back so he could come in. "But there's a slight change in plans. I'm running late, so I called out for some food. I hope you like pizza." She waved a hand toward the kitchen. "There are drinks in the fridge, help yourself to whatever you want. I'm going up to take a shower, and while you're waiting you can look at these." She hesitated for an instant before scooping up a pile of drawings and handing them to him.

His dark brows lifted. "Yours?"

"Mine." She nodded wearily. "I've been at it since I got home, and I finished about five minutes ago. So, my part's done, Luke. Now it's up to you." She turned and started climbing the stairs.

"Megan?" His voice was rough with concern.

She stopped and looked over her shoulder. "Don't worry," she said with a tired smile. "I'm fine. I'll be back, and then we'll talk. About everything. I'll be down before the pizza gets here."

A minute later, she was in the shower letting the rush of water pummel her stiff shoulders. It never changed when she entered those old houses, she thought, sagging against the cool tiles. Impressions battering at her, a new one super-imposing itself over the remnants of the previous one. An awareness of people from the past, their clothing, their activities, the rooms they lived in.

Then, with the last image dissolving, there was the urgency to get it all on paper, the driving need to record it before the details faded, the emotions flagged. It was like being caught up in a whirlwind, sucked dry and then dropped, emptied and exhausted.

Her maternal grandmother, who had dealt with a similar type of "sight," had called it a magnificent passion. It was a gift, she maintained stoutly, to be cherished. As always, after being wrung dry, Megan wondered why it seemed more like a curse.

But when she looked back at the houses she had restored—a legacy of history to the present from the past—she had no doubts. It *was* a gift, pure and simple. It was just a gift that was occasionally difficult to deal with.

Thinking of the evening stretching ahead of her, Megan stepped out of the shower and swore again. She was too tired to deal with a left-brained, linear thinker who didn't believe in much more than he could see and touch.

What was more, she was in no condition to deflect the surges of emotion he blasted her with at the most unexpected moments. The fact that he didn't know he was doing it didn't change the results. It was still like holding a lightning bolt in her bare hand.

Wrapping a towel around her hair like a turban, she walked to the closet and looked for something that might diffuse the electricity that kicked in every time they were together. Something innocuous. It shouldn't be too hard, she reflected, reaching for white slacks and a matching tunic. Her wardrobe didn't run along seductive lines. A few gold chains and earrings completed the outfit.

She was walking down the stairs just as someone knuckled a brisk tattoo on the door. "I'll get it," she called to Luke. Shrugging when there was no response, she opened the door. "Casey! What are you doing here?"

A tall blond man with laughing green eyes gently swung a flat box beneath her nose. "Delivering. One humongous pizza, with everything except anchovies, and a salad, as ordered."

"You shouldn't be doing this—you own the place, remember?" She grinned at him. She couldn't help it. She always did. "You're supposed to be cracking the whip, stirring the slaves into action, not standing on my doorstep."

"When my favorite—" he cocked a brow at the scowling man who had materialized behind her, draping a possessive arm around her shoulder "—lady orders one of my pizzas, the least I can do is make sure she gets it."

Megan sighed, knowing exactly what he was doing. "You're impossible. Always were and always will be. What's the deal here? How much do I owe you? Do I tip the owner?"

"The pizza's on the house." He gave her a provoking grin. "A kiss will cover the delivery."

A five-dollar bill appeared over Megan's shoulder with some grim advice. "Don't push it, friend."

Megan laughed and snatched at the bill. "Don't encourage him."

The blond was quicker. He grabbed the money and thrust the pizza at her. "Thanks. Will I see you on Saturday?"

The grip on Megan's shoulder tightened. Trying to ignore it, as well as the accompanying jolt of pure masculine stake-claiming, she nodded. "Yes. You and your wife and your daughters will see me on Saturday, cousin."

He grinned again. "Good." He gave another quick glance behind her. "Devin told me to report back with any interesting news."

Megan sighed. "And?"

"From where I stand, it looks ominous. But interesting. So I'll call."

"Traitor."

He leaned forward and gave her a quick peck on the cheek. "Just the family net closing in, babe. See you Saturday." He took off at a lope and left Megan holding the pizza and salad.

She stepped back into the wall of warm muscle. Before she could retreat, large hands settled at her waist, lifted her effortlessly and turned her away from the door.

"Food," she said shakily, heading for the kitchen.

"Right." Luke followed her. "Where do you keep the plates?" Snagging them out of the cupboard she pointed to, he asked mildly, "Who's Devin?"

"One of my brothers." Megan handed him a tray with salads and napkins, grabbed the pizza and headed back to the living room. "My twin."

"Protective?"

"Very."

"And the cousin? Is he always like that?"

Megan nodded. "Females are at a premium in the Murphy clan. In my generation there are three out of eighteen, so the males—brothers, cousins, uncles—have a tendency to throw up a protective fence around the women in the family. Whether we need it or not."

Whether we want it or not.

Settling on one end of the rattan sofa, she motioned for him to sit beside her and put the tray on the glass-topped table. "Food first," she ordered, opening the box. "Then talk."

Luke was working on his third slice when he paused. "Am I allowed to tell you how much I like the drawings?" Her mouth was full, but her eyes widened, and he watched in satisfaction as the look of strain left them.

She swallowed and said thickly, "Enough?"

"For what?"

"To give me free rein? To do the job without sticking those blasted flowers of yours on the walls?"

"You never give up, do you?" He caught a piece of pepperoni with his teeth before it slid off onto his tan slacks, then watched Megan grapple with strings of cheese.

"Nope." She shook her head. "I don't."

"Are you always this stubborn?"

"Yep." She turned slightly to face him. "I have to be. There aren't that many people left who know what the old places look like. If we're going to preserve part of our history for the next generations, even in commercial buildings, it has to be done now, and it has to be done right. Here, have some more."

The truce ended when Luke finished the last piece and folded the box. "Exactly who are you?" he asked quietly.

Megan's smile was wry. "Don't you mean *what* am I?"

He shrugged. "Okay, let's try it that way."

"I'm a perfectly normal woman who happens to be just a wee bit...psychic."

Luke's brows rose. "You really do read minds?"

"That's not what I meant," she said with a scowl. "But, well, yes, as a matter of fact, I do. Sometimes. Rarely. Not intentionally. And not with everyone. Just certain people who...send things quite strongly."

"You're saying that at your house that first day, I was—"

Megan nodded. "Yes. You were."

Luke swore softly, succinctly.

Megan waited, giving him a chance to absorb what she had said. He didn't like it. Not one little bit. She knew it as surely as she knew matters were only going to get worse. Luke was a man who played his cards close to his chest. She would bet her next commission that he rarely discussed options with business associates. He made decisions, gave orders and expected them to be followed.

He was a private man and would definitely not like the idea that she could traipse in and out of his mind practically at will. And he would hate the fact that while he kept his poker face intact she would be attuned to the emotions surging through him.

Of course, there was no law that said he *had* to know everything at once, she reminded herself. The government, in its wisdom, had a name for just such a situation. It was called revealing information on a need-to-know basis. Yes, she reflected, Luke would definitely be a happier man if she didn't dump all of this on him at once.

She gave him a rueful look, hoping it would be soothing. "Unfortunately for both of us, transmitting or receiving messages of this sort isn't always voluntary. Or predictable."

"So you just walked into my head?"

"No." Her sympathy vanished at the sarcastic question. "You make it sound as if I were bored and decided to go for a stroll. It wasn't that way at all. You were shouting things at me and I couldn't avoid hearing them."

Stunned, he began, "I was sh—"

She held up a hand to stop him. "Yes, you were. Look, it's not unusual for me to pick up feelings from other people. That happens a lot, and I've learned to deflect most of them." She eyed him uncertainly. "I don't know how to explain it. After a while I just learned not to pay attention."

Luke stared at her in wary fascination.

"It doesn't happen all the time," she assured him. "It comes and goes. Most of the time, you're perfectly safe behind that poker face—I haven't the foggiest idea what you're thinking. The only person I consistently read that clearly is Devin."

This was definitely one of the need-to-know times, she decided. It wouldn't make Luke feel any better to know that she and Devin were psychically linked. That wherever they were, regardless of how far apart they were, they always knew when the other was dealing with an emotional situation. That they could feel the emotions.

Nor did he want to know that when they were with each other, their thoughts were frequently as audible as spoken words. And that she had never reacted to anyone else the same way. Until now.

It wasn't unusual for the twins to have intuitive knowledge of a situation. The family had long since become inured to the fact. They even expected it. But they would all be astonished if they knew she was picking up another man's thoughts with the same ease with which she read Devin's. They would be more than astounded, she reflected uneasily. They would be downright speculative, and the last thing she needed was to have her family start matchmaking. Especially when the man in question was Lucas McCall.

"You see," she continued in a rush, "basically, I have historic cognition. I see things in the past quite clearly."

"Hist—"

She nodded.

Luke frowned. "Wait a minute. Let me get this straight. Exactly how much research did you do before we went out to the plantation?"

Megan's first finger and thumb met in a circle. "Zippo." She gave a slight shrug. "There wasn't anything to do. I've checked out your places before. They aren't listed in any books, there are no plans on file anywhere, and there aren't any in-depth articles in our local magazines."

"What about the cottages? You were so sure they were behind the house."

"I still am. I felt them as soon as I got out of the truck. I'll bet if we go back, we'll find the founda—"

"I already did."

Megan blinked. "You found them," she began slowly, "and didn't *say* anything? How could you—"

"How was I supposed to know you'd be interested? You sounded pretty certain to me."

"Oh. Yeah. I guess I did." Turning the conversation back to the point that interested her most, she said, casually, "So you like the drawings?"

Luke picked them up and riffled through them. "You're the psychic in the crowd. You tell me."

She nodded complacently. "You liked them."

"You're right. They have just the touch I wanted—old-world charm, spacious rooms, simplicity and warmth. And I like the idea of the extra bungalows. The ones placed where the original foundations just happen to be," he added dryly. "So, we'll go with them and the logo you designed."

"But?" she prompted, watching his eyes.

"I thought you were so big on authenticity."

"I am."

"The existing structure doesn't look much like the overgrown grass shack you've drawn."

Megan sighed. "I know. All I can say is, I tried several sketches based on the present house and it just wouldn't work. It always came out like this." She gave a slight shrug. "Based on past experience, I can say with some certainty that this is the way it looked originally."

"*Some* certainty?"

"Some. I'll know more before we get too far, and if I'm wrong I'll change them."

Luke stared at her thoughtfully, then nodded. "Okay, now I'd like you to start at the beginning and tell me how you did them."

Megan stiffened.

"You said you didn't do any research and that you're an historic cognizant, whatever the hell that is. I want to know how you come up with your ideas."

"The results are the only thing that matters," she mut-tered stubbornly. "No one ever asks me how I do it."

"I'm different. I don't go into things blind. Start talk-ing."

"Oh, for heaven's sake," she grumbled.

"Now, Megan."

"I'm just...sensitive to old things," she finally said with an annoyed shrug. "When I walk into these plantation homes I'm bombarded with images."

"And?" He waited.

"It's not always the same. Sometimes just walking through the room is enough. Other times, I touch things that belong to the original structure—wall, doorways, win-dows, floors."

"And you just close your eyes and concentrate," he fin-ished dryly.

Megan brightened. "Exactly." Her smile dimmed as she studied his skeptical expression. "You don't believe me, do you?"

"Let's put it this way. I find it hard to believe that some-one with your reputation does her research simply by walk-ing around with her eyes closed."

Her eyes narrowed.

"Of course, there is the fact that you were sitting on the kitchen floor this morning," he said thoughtfully. "But I don't know for sure what you were doing there. For all I know, you were communing with the banyan tree." He gave a negligent shrug. "I suppose the bottom line is that I like your ideas and the new logo. I want to discuss some of the rooms, but I won't interfere. You've got the job if you want it. And if anyone ever asks, your story would be great pub-licity."

Torn between excitement and fury, she opted for anger. She would celebrate getting the job later. The blasted man didn't believe her. "That *story*," she said fiercely, "just happens to be true, and until tonight no one outside of my family knew about it. It's not a juicy tidbit for the papers, *Mis*ter McCall. In fact—"

"Luke."

"—it's the reason I go to new sites by myself. I always have the strongest reaction the first time there." She surged to her feet, working off her fury by pacing the length of the room. "Damn it, I *knew* it was a mistake to go with you today. I never go with clients, and I don't know why I let you talk me into it."

Luke stayed where he was, watching her stalk and fume. When she turned, touching a chair back, he was reminded of something she'd said the day they met.

"On top of all this—" he waved a hand to encompass her revelations— "you're a healer? Doesn't that keep you pretty busy?"

He hadn't meant the question to be offensive—he was simply trying to work his way through the confusion—but he wasn't surprised when she took it the wrong way.

"Don't hassle me, McCall. I explained that. My family calls me a healer, but I don't buy into it. I just have a knack for massage. When I mentioned it, it was just a stupid comment to take your mind off what you were obviously thinking."

When she came up for air, he said, "Does this stuff really run in your family?"

Her blue eyes blazed at him. "Don't start on my relatives! They're wonderful. Full of love...and laughter. So what if they have a few quirks? Lots of people do. There's nothing wrong with—"

He looked at her, astounded. "It does, doesn't it? It runs right through your whole—"

"Not all of them," she said through gritted teeth. "Just a few. A special few. Why are you suddenly so interested in my family?" she demanded.

"I don't know," he said honestly. "I just thought it might help me understand what I'm dealing with here."

"You're dealing with *me.*"

"I know. And you're driving me crazy with all this hocus pocus."

Megan stared down at him, her fists resting aggressively on her hips. "All right. You want to know about my family? See the rest of the loonies? Fine. What are you doing Saturday night?"

Four

Music and conversation drifted through the balmy darkness as Megan and Luke climbed the stairs to her parents' house.

She should have been more specific when she told him dress was casual, she reflected, taking a quick sideways glance at Luke. With the sleeves of his light blue shirt rolled up his forearms, and his darker blue slacks and polished loafers, he still resembled an off-duty executive. He was going to stand out like a raven among parakeets when he mingled with the rest of the party, she reflected wryly. Especially since thongs, shorts, pareaus or sarongs and wild Hawaiian shirts were the order of the day.

I have to be crazy.

Inviting him to one of the monthly family nights was either insanity or rank stupidity. If he wasn't overcome by the sheer number of bodies, he'd probably have second thoughts about their bargain after meeting some of her relatives.

Well, that *was* the idea—even if the invitation had been extended when her wits were scattered by rage. If he was going to change his mind because of a few psychic oddities, better now than later.

But if I'm really lucky, he'll simply be so distracted by the others that he won't get any more curious about me than he already is.

Megan pushed open the gate at the end of the patio and looked over her shoulder. "Ready?"

"Good God, is this all family?" Luke scanned the milling crowd, absorbing the genetic jumble ranging from blondes and redheads to black-eyed islanders.

"Ummm-hmm." Satisfaction made the sound a purr. "Every last one of them. Is it so different from yours?"

"A bit," he said laconically. "I was the only child of parents who were the same." And they had been too busy climbing the economic and social ladders to concern themselves with family gatherings and entertaining a small boy.

Megan looked up at him, stunned. "You have no cousins? No aunts and uncles?"

He gave her a slow smile. "Don't look so worried. I survived."

She didn't look convinced, but having learned that his physical impact was diluted when his mind was occupied, she hooked her arm through his and urged him forward, keeping up a running commentary while she looked for her parents.

"Then this must seem like a real zoo to you. Years ago, my father and his two brothers left Ireland and settled here. Each married an island girl and raised a large, colorful brood. Eighteen kids in all, seven in my family. By now, many of them have married and have kids of their own. I gave up counting a long time ago.''

"I can see why."

Luke gazed around appreciatively. The house, remodeled in stages, was more a Polynesian fantasy compound than a family residence. A winding patio led from the house to the pool, past miniature waterfalls, cascading fountains, ponds and lacy ferns. Lawn furniture with plump cushions provided bright conversational areas along the way.

"Nice place."

Megan grinned. "My dad leans toward the flamboyant. Oh, there they are." She led him toward a redheaded giant who was towering over a serene, dark-eyed woman.

Luke watched as Megan gave each of them an enthusiastic hug.

Both women were about five foot four inches, which meant that their heads just reached his shoulder. Both were slim, arranged their hair in one long braid and wore clinging sarongs that left their shoulders bare.

That was where the similarities ended. Megan's mother had black hair barely touched with silver, a slow smile and a lavender dress. Megan had her father's coloring—hair like dark fire and incredible blue eyes. Her frequent smile came fast and warmed everyone within ten feet.

Her dress—a pareau, she had informed him earlier—was nothing more than a strip of green fabric with large white flowers. It should be outlawed, Luke thought for the tenth time since he had knocked on her door. It was pure temptation, making a man wonder where it began and ended—and how quickly he could get her out of it.

Megan was a toucher—except when she was alone with him. It was obviously a trait shared by the rest of the family. More times than he had bothered to count, their walk across the patio had been interrupted by family members who greeted Megan as if they hadn't seen her in months. They had hugged her, kissed her on the cheek, draped an arm around her shoulders to hold her close or merely clasped hands while they spoke.

After planting a quick kiss on her father's cheek, she reached out to tug at Luke's sleeve, bringing him closer. "Mom, Dad, this is Luke McCall, the owner of the plantations I told you about. Luke, my parents, Sean and Mei Murphy."

"Glad you two finally got together on this project," Sean rumbled, shaking Luke's hand briskly. "With your money and my girl's talent, you'll have a place to be proud of."

"I'm very happy to meet you, Luke. Megan has told us about—" Mei touched Luke's hand and came to an abrupt halt, blinking. She cast a quick glance at Megan as her fingers tightened around his. "You are always welcome at our house, Luke," she said slowly. "Always. Come back soon."

She turned to Megan, touching her shoulder with gentle fingers. "Have you seen Uncle Loe yet?"

Megan shook her head with a bit more force than was necessary.

"See that Luke meets him."

"What was that all about?" Luke asked, after her parents wandered away to mingle with the other guests.

"You don't want to know, believe me." Megan shivered, thinking of her mother's uncanny aptitude for what her irreverent offspring called "reading vibes." Long before others spotted it, she had been aware of the psychic link that transformed two individuals into a couple. While Mei's record wasn't perfect, her success rate was very high.

"Forwarned is forearmed," he muttered.

You betcha. "I guess." Megan hesitated, then lifted her shoulders in a damn-the-torpedoes shrug. Nudging him slightly to the right, she directed him along a torch-lit path to the pool.

"All right. The good news is that Uncle Loe is a kahuna."

"What the heck's a kahuna?"

"That's also part of the bad news."

He led her to a small padded bench and sat down, bringing her down beside him. "Are you going to tell me this straight out, or do I have to pry it out of you?"

Megan sighed. "Some people call a kahuna a priest, some a shaman, some a—"

Luke groaned. "Witch doctor, right?" When she remained silent, he leaned back, crossing his arms on his chest. "Okay, why does your mother want me to meet a witch doctor?"

"A kahuna," she said with deliberation. "Because Uncle Loe blesses things." And his other specialty was wedding ceremonies. But this time, her mother was dead wrong.

"Right." He settled deeper into the seat. "And I need something blessed?"

She nodded. "As a matter of fact, you do—the bed and breakfast, when it's done."

"Tell me you're kidding." When she just looked at him, he sighed. "You're not. Okay, I'll bite. Why?"

"Because that's the way things are done."

"I hate to tell you this, honey, but I have four hotels open and running and I've never even heard of this thing."

"A blessing. And you've never opened one in Hawaii."

"What'll happen if I don't have it done?" His expression was one she was getting used to—fascinated but wary.

She shrugged, wondering about his level of tolerance. Hoping it was high, she said, "Bad luck. People might not come. If they do, they might hear or see things that frighten them."

"What kind of things?"

"Ghosts." She grinned at his pained expression.

Luke briefly closed his eyes. When he opened them, her smile had faded and was replaced by a worried look in her blue eyes. "Do you really believe that?"

Her gaze didn't quite meet his when she replied. "Here on the islands, our old people are very important to us. They tell stories of many strange things that have happened when people didn't observe the customs."

"That doesn't answer my question."

"For heaven's sake, Luke! I'm twenty-six. I have a college education and I live in the modern world."

He grinned at her flustered expression. "You're also beating around the bush, sweetheart. Give me a straight answer."

"Do I believe? Yes. Absolutely." She waved an agitated hand. "And no. Positively."

"Couldn't be straighter than that," he murmured, capturing her hand and holding it in his.

"What I do is hedge my bets," she finally said with a sigh. "I believe what the old people say. At least, I believe *they* believe it. And I've seen some weird things happen when places aren't blessed. Business losses, things that I can't explain. Things that are changed when the place *is* blessed. So, it just isn't worth being stubborn about. Every business has a grand opening of some sort, every home has a housewarming."

She took her gaze off their linked fingers long enough to give him an anxious look. "So when the time comes, I strongly urge my clients to include a blessing in the festivities."

Luke got to his feet and tugged her up beside him. "Then maybe we should have a chat with your Uncle Loe."

"You've been hard to find lately, Sunshine."

Megan turned and flung herself into the arms of the man who had murmured the words. "Devin! I wondered where you were."

"Just wandering around, saying hello to everyone."

Luke watched as Devin dropped a soft kiss on her fiery hair. Even if she hadn't called him by name, he would have had no doubts. He was looking at the twin. A man as essentially masculine as his sister was feminine, yet with the same features, hair and eyes.

For an instant Devin held his sister in a tight embrace. Before he released her, he looked directly into Luke's eyes. His gaze, Luke realized with a slight sense of surprise, held recognition. It was also a blend of curiosity, humor and warning, not the distinct challenge he had expected.

Wrapping a long arm around Megan's waist, Devin said, "I understand you're looking for Uncle Loe. I'll keep your friend company while you go find him." His smile was bland.

Megan blinked and gave him a worried frown. "Devin." The word was sharp with warning. "I don't want you—" She broke off when he lifted his shoulders in an innocent shrug.

"What?"

"Don't 'what' me. You behave."

"Don't I always?"

"No, you don't," she said crossly. She darted an anxious glance at Luke and found that he was smiling with genuine amusement. "I haven't even introduced you."

"We know who we are," Devin assured her, grinning at her frustrated scowl. "Go on, Sunshine. We aren't going anywhere."

She turned a harried glance to Luke.

Keeping his eyes on Devin, Luke reached out and cupped her bare shoulder with his large hand, deliberately stroking her smooth skin with his thumb, watching her brother's eyes narrow. "Go find your uncle," he said mildly. "We'll be right here, waiting for you."

The two men watched her walk away, each waiting for the other to break the charged silence.

"My sister is a very special woman," Devin said quietly.

Luke nodded.

"She's very important to me."

"I figured that out before I met you."

"And to my family."

"I've seen that tonight."

"She spreads joy as easily as the sun gives light."

They watched as a long arm snagged Megan around the waist and drew her into a cluster of boisterous teenagers. One of them tugged lightly at her braid. Both men smiled when she said something that caused a ripple of laughter to spread through the group.

"She can't survive away from the island," Devin said conversationally. "Don't try to take her."

Luke's brows rose. "Is that a warning?"

"No, it's a statement of fact. Her heart and soul are here. She tried to leave twice—once to go to school, once for a man. Both times she…withered. Both times she came back. She won't leave again."

With his gaze still on Megan's vivid face, Luke said, "What's the rest? You didn't come over here just to keep me company."

Devin turned away from watching his sister to face Luke. "I think we could be friends. I'd like that. But that will only happen if Megan stays happy. If you take away her laughter, I'll kill you. *That's* my warning."

Megan had worked her way around the patio and was joining a group when she spotted a familiar head of curly gray hair. She gave him a quick peck on his lean, tan cheek and neatly cut him out of the herd, shepherding him toward the men at the far end of the patio. "Uncle Loe, there's someone I want you to meet."

"What took you so long? We've all had a fine time watching the sparks fly between you two this evening. When's the wedding?"

Aghast, she spun around to face him and came to a dead stop. "Don't say that! Not even as a joke."

The skin around his eyes crinkled as he smiled. "Who's kidding? Not me."

"We've only known each other a few days!"

He shrugged philosophically. "It happens that way sometimes. Especially in this family."

"Well, that's not the case this time." Her voice took on an urgent note as Luke and Devin strolled their way. "All I want you to do is explain a blessing to my new client. A *blessing,* Uncle Loe. Try to get his approval for one and then stop. No talking about what a nice girl I am, no discussing weddings. Nothing else."

Her voice rose in a gay tone that had all three men raising their brows. "Luke! Devin! Look who I found. Luke, come meet my uncle."

When the introductions were over, Devin took her arm and stepped aside. "Why don't we walk down and take a look at the pool?"

Megan groaned. "Not you, too. Everyone I've talked to tonight wants to know about Luke."

"Don't worry, I'm not going to pick your brain." He laced his fingers through hers, urging her forward. "I know as much as I need to know."

"Like what?" she asked in alarm.

"That he's a self-made man, for starters. In danger of becoming a workaholic—or, at least, he was before he met you. He wants the best, but he's willing to work or pay for it. He also wants you. How's that for a thumbnail sketch?''

She stared broodingly into the depths of the lighted pool. "I told you that last part already. I also said he didn't want to want me."

"I think you're right. My impression is that he feels that way about everyone. For what it's worth, my advice is to steer clear of him. He's locked up an important part of himself and tossed away the key."

"That would be the sensible thing," she agreed.

"But you're not going to do it."

Megan shivered. "I think it's already gone beyond that. It's crazy, Dev. I hardly know him, but there's something that..." She paused. "He saw me at work in the old house the other day."

Devin whistled between his teeth. Dropping his arm across her shoulders, he said, "And?"

"He doesn't know what to believe. He's trying to decide whether I'm simply weird or a weird liar. He said my story would make great publicity."

"Well, hell." He gave her a quick hug. "Want me to break a few of his bones?''

She smiled, as he had intended. "No. I want you to let your big sister work it out, all by herself."

"I've got a bad feeling about this, Sunshine." His arm tightened, drawing her closer. "This guy can hurt you."

She rested her hand on his and squeezed. "Luke wouldn't do that."

"Not deliberately. That's not what I'm talking about. I'd hand him his head on a platter if he did." He shook his head impatiently. "It's not that."

Megan waited, allowing him to collect his thoughts.

"Meggie, I wish you weren't working with him. I wish you'd call the whole thing off."

She shook her head. "Not on your life. I'd wait a life-time for another chance like this."

"I'm not talking about your job, for God's sake. I'm talking about you. This guy could eat you for breakfast and never even burp."

"Don't be silly."

"I'm not. I'm being worried. First, last and always, Luke McCall is a businessman. He does everything by the book."

She gave him a look of pure exasperation. "Devin, I don't know what on earth you're talking about."

"Don't get involved with him, Sunshine. Do your job, work with him, but don't go beyond that. Don't open up your soft heart, because he won't. I don't think he knows anything about love—how to give *or* receive it."

Megan blinked. "Who's talking about love?"

"I am." Devin's voice was grim. "And I hope to God I'm wrong."

Several hours later, Megan leaned back against the silver cushions and watched Luke's large hands on the steering wheel. He drove the way he did everything else—compe-tently, without fuss.

"Well," she asked as he pulled to a stop in her drive, "what do you think? Are we all loony, or just some of us?"

"And do you still beat your wife?" he mocked softly, his gaze on her teasing smile. "What I think is that you hoped your family would distract me." He opened his door and looked over his shoulder at her. "Honey, I don't care if they dance naked in the moonlight to bagpipe music or worship trees. I want to know what makes you tick. *You,* just you."

Megan scrambled out and met him at the front of the car. "Do you, uh, want a cup of coffee?"

"No," he said with barely controlled violence. "What I want is you. If I come in, I won't leave until morning. Is that what you want?"

Her stunned expression told him that it wasn't. At least, not yet.

Luke framed her face with his big hands, pinning her against the fender. "I want to taste you. Your lips have been driving me crazy since the first time I saw you. I want to know if they're as soft as they look."

Megan's gasp of surprise was a sharp sound in the still night air. "I . . . told you that first day I wasn't interested," she whispered after a long moment.

"You lied."

Of course she had, but that was neither here nor there. "Luke, this isn't a smart thing to do. It will only complicate matters," she said a bit desperately as he lowered his head.

His grin flashed in the darkness. "What with ghosts and witch doctors running around, I don't think it can get more complicated. It's just a kiss, honey. That's all we're talking about."

His breath was warm on her lips. "You can stop me. All you have to do is say no, but I think you're as curious as I am. As hungry as I am." He waited a long moment, grateful for the moonlight illuminating her expressive face.

Caution gave way to curiosity and, finally, a sweet, feminine impatience that made the blood roar through his veins. When she lifted her face to his, he slid his hands down her body, cupping her bottom, fitting her against him.

His lips touched hers softly, testing, tasting, in direct contrast to the urgency that was flowing from him, ensnaring her. Megan could feel the heat of his body, the flex of muscles as he drew her closer, the controlled strength of his hands.

Control. Scorching heat. Desire. Determination. His emotions swamped her as his lips became hot and demanding. His mouth absorbed her soft sound of surprise, pleasure.

Megan twisted in his arms, moving nearer still, instinctively responding to his hunger, his need. *Her* need. She slid her fingers through his thick hair, holding him close.

Closer.

Until she couldn't think. Only feel. Respond. Burn in his arms. Want more. And know that she would shatter if she didn't get away.

When she made a soft protest and pressed her hand against his shoulder, she could feel his control kick in. It was touch and go for a long moment, then he stiffened and moved back, touching her hair with fingers that shook.

Megan took a deep, shaky breath as she leaned back against the fender, her arms sliding down around his waist. Holding him loosely, she rested her forehead against his chest. Finally, when her heart quit its frantic pounding, she broke the electric silence with a shaky laugh. "For just a kiss, that was pretty shattering."

"Yeah." Luke's voice reeked with masculine satisfaction.

"Luke," Megan began cautiously, "this is nothing to play with."

"Who's playing?" He lifted her, settling her on the fender in a shaft of moonlight where he could see her more clearly. Wrapping an arm around her bare shoulders, he felt every ragged breath she took.

"What I mean is, we have a big job ahead of us, and—"

"And what?" His voice sharpened.

"And maybe we should just stick to business," she finished with a rush.

Luke looked at her in disbelief. "You're kidding, right?"

She shook her head.

"After a kiss like that—" he moved his thumb in a gentle stroke across her tender lips "—you can say let's forget it and get back to work?"

"I didn't say it would be easy, just . . . sensible."

"And impossible," he said flatly. "Sweetheart, you're the mind reader here. It seems like you'd have it all figured out by now."

"What?"

"That this is just the beginning."

Five
___

This is just the beginning.

Luke's words seemed to echo in the silence of the room, as they had so often in the last few days. It didn't take much to bring them back, Megan admitted in a spasm of honesty. She thought of them every time she saw Luke, every time his gaze met hers, every time he breathed.

Hell, every time *she* breathed.

"What do you think about thatched roofs on the bungalows?" she asked hurriedly, to break the treacherous train of thought. Looking up from her sketch pad, she waited for Luke's response. She wasn't sure she really wanted his opinion, but it was better than brooding over his threat. Or promise.

It was odd having him here, she thought, her breath catching as his dark gaze settled on her. And unnerving.

He lounged casually on a chair beside her large worktable, long legs stretched out comfortably, crossed at the ankles. He didn't look like a man with four hotels to his credit, she mused. Or one who probably terrorized the various members of his staff. What he did look like was a man. All man.

The fabric of Luke's pale blue shirt stretched over his wide shoulders and was open far enough at the neck to reveal the same crisp, dark hair that dusted his arms. Soft, worn jeans hugged his lean hips and muscular thighs. His running shoes were scuffed. After observing her work outfits of shorts and knit shirts, he had obviously decided to go with the island flow, she thought with a grin.

The first day after her parents' party, they had tried working at their own places, using the phone for the endless consultations. It had been an awkward arrangement, so the next day she had dragged her equipment to his suite. Now, four days later, they were working at her house, sharing her office.

Luke blinked, focusing on her. "Hmm?"

"Bungalows?" She waggled the drawing in front of him. "Thatched roofs?"

"You mean I get a choice?"

She gave him a patient look. "Don't be provoking. When there are several options, all equally viable, you always get a choice. So, what do you think? Fire-treated cane wears well, and it's certainly authentic."

"Is that your preference?" When she nodded, he said, "Let's go with it, then," and returned his attention to the model of the plantation he was constructing from her drawings.

She grinned again, remembering his reaction when she'd offered to have the task done professionally. Disappointment had flickered in his dark eyes, then sheer determination. No, he wanted to do it.

It made her think of a kid turned loose with a set of Tinkertoys, except for a couple of major differences. Luke was a skilled craftsman doing a top-notch job. And he was no kid. He had also carefully pointed out that his trip was part business, part vacation, so he could select his own entertainment.

"You're good at that," she said idly, sketching in the thatched roofs.

"I should be." He wielded a sharp knife with casual expertise, skimming it down the trunk of the monkeypod tree he was shaping. "I'm a carpenter."

"Right. And I'm a first-year art student."

He nodded absently. "It's true. At least, that's how I started. Then I got my contractor's license, built a few houses on spec just as the market was at an all-time high. The rest, as they say, is history. I invested some money, made some and got into hotels."

"That simple, huh?" She snapped her fingers. "Just like that?"

He held up the tree and eyed it critically. "More or less."

"Sure. What about your parents?"

"What about them?" His even tone shut off that part of his life as effectively as a spiked fence and a troop of slathering dobermans.

Megan shrugged and said carefully, "I just wondered if they were in the construction business."

"No."

Smudging dark streaks on the cane roof, she took a quick sideways glance at his bent head. No. End of subject. She'd seen it done before but never better. Luke had a definite talent with one-syllable words. It could be a handy thing to learn.

The arrangement was working fairly well, she reflected, returning to her original thought—at least, on the surface.

It was the tension humming underneath that was driving her crazy.

Mornings, Luke worked in his hotel suite, doing whatever it was that hotel tycoons did. She appeared early each afternoon to resume work on the model, as well as to be available to discuss the more detailed drawings she was working on. Dinner was a joint effort or they had food delivered to the house. Then it was back to business, which meant they spent the evenings together.

But never the nights.

And it was that issue that was causing her to lose sleep, Megan admitted to herself crossly. The nights. Nights that were long, restless and, for someone who had spent most of them in relatively solitary contentment, surprisingly lonely.

Nights that gave her too much time to think.

At the beginning of a new job, her mind was usually blissfully chaotic, a tumble of electrifying possibilities energizing her for the work ahead. The sky seemed bluer, the air headier, the flowers bloomed for her alone. It was, as the song said, like being in love.

Now, in one way, it was much the same. Colors were brighter, the air was like champagne, and something wonderful, it seemed, was about to happen. On the downside, there were times when the electricity thrumming between the two of them was almost unbearable. And that, she brooded gloomily, was probably also like being in love.

Love.

It was on her mind a lot these days, a topic her family regularly waxed eloquent on—many of them taking a stand on the side of love at first sight. Mei, of course, was the leading proponent. All it should take, she lectured, was one look. One meeting if you were slow.

Megan jumped to her feet, muttering when she hit her knee on the corner of the desk. She was going stir-crazy, she decided. Love—baloney. What she felt was the result of nothing more than too much togetherness and too little exercise.

Luke looked up. "What's the matter?"

"Nothing." *Everything.* "I have to go out to the plantation for a while."

"Why?"

Megan eyed him thoughtfully. "There are just some things I have to check. I want to...get the feel of the place again. Usually there's too much coming at me the first time to absorb it all. It shouldn't take me long."

She shook her head as he put down the carving. "No, don't get up. No need to stop what you're doing. I'll just zip out there and—"

"I'll go with you."

She gave him an exasperated glance. "Luke, watch my lips. I'm a big girl. I've been doing this for a long time. Alone. All by myself. Solo."

"I know." He folded the knife and slid it in the pocket of his jeans. "And you know I bought the place as is because I was interested primarily in the land. The house has been empty for a long time and the termites have had a field day. You can have all the privacy you want, but you're not going alone. You go with me, or you don't go."

And that was apparently that, she thought, still fuming a few minutes later as the black truck jounced over the rutted road.

When he pulled up in front of the house, she jumped out and smoothed her white shorts. "I don't know how long I'll be."

His brows rose at her testy tone. "Whatever," he said mildly. "I'll be under the banyan tree. Whittling."

He grinned when she just scowled and stalked into the house. The legend was definitely not amused.

Tough.

Megan wasn't going to risk her neck on his property, on his time. As far as that went, she wasn't going to risk her neck, period. Not if he had anything to say about it. And in this case, he did.

She left the door open as he had instructed. She probably wasn't happy about that, either, he reflected grimly. That was also tough. He was willing to give her all the time alone she needed to commune with spooks, but he would damn well be where he could hear her if she called out.

Luke sat at the foot of the banyan, leaning against the trunk, watching for movement in the doorway while he thought about her crazy story. Historic cognition. He'd had four days to mull it over, and he still didn't know what to think. His first instinct had been to give her credit for a great imagination. His second had warned him about the first. Since he'd never dealt with ESP or any of its shirttail relatives, he hadn't given the subject much thought, and even now, thrown headfirst into the matter, nose to nose with mind reading and kahunas, he still didn't know how credible it all was.

All he knew for sure was that Megan believed every word she'd uttered.

Late-afternoon shadows threw stark images on the grass by the time Megan joined him.

Luke's eyes narrowed as she dropped down beside him. "You look beat."

She nodded. "I always am when I do this. At least, when I start a project. It's draining."

"I don't like it." His voice was abrupt.

"I'm not always crazy about it myself." She gave him a tired smile, then lay back, resting her head on her hands.

Luke waited, watching her slowly relax. When she began dreamily studying the sky through the canopy of leaves overhead, he broke the silence.

"Well, did you . . . learn anything?"

Her brows rose as she considered the question and the tone in which it was asked. "Did you know that when many of these old homes were built, in the late eighteen-sixties and seventies, there were no hotels?" she asked idly. "They built very large homes, and visitors to the island—at least, those with connections—were passed from one place to another as guests."

"A practical arrangement."

"Mmm-hmm. Most of the early settlers were New Englanders who built the types of homes they were accustomed to—with small windows protecting them from winter winds. Of course, they sweltered in them over here."

She sat up, her blue eyes sparkling with excitement. "But this man was different. He was a New Englander, too, but—"

"Which man?"

"The man who built this place." She waved an impatient hand toward the house. "I was right about the original structure—and the man. He was flexible enough to take the best of both cultures. He built the place with good, old-fashioned Yankee durability, but in the Hawaiian style. It had a sloping thatched roof, deep eaves and a porch all the way around. Big windows took advantage of the breezes, while archways and high ceilings kept the spacious rooms looking light and cool."

"Megan—"

She held up her hands, palms facing him. "Don't say it. I know. The jury's still out as far as you're concerned. You'd feel a lot better if I could bring you a book or a set of plans telling you this story. You don't know if I'm weird or crazy, and you're not sure which you'd prefer, right?''

"I just—"

"That's okay, I understand."

"No, I don't think—"

"Yes." She nodded. "I do. Luke, I've spent most of my life getting looks like the one you're giving me now. You don't have to look so grim," she said, grinning at him. "You've been exposed to a concentrated dose of this stuff. It's a bit like changing altitude—it takes a while to adjust."

She jumped to her feet and held out a hand to him. "Come on. I need to get back to the drawing board."

An instant before his long fingers clamped around her wrist, she knew she had made a mistake. Luke wasn't distracted this time. On the contrary. His attention was as concentrated as a laser beam—and it was aimed directly at her.

This is just the beginning.

The words flew through her mind as she tumbled down and sprawled across Luke's lap. For a moment, she didn't feel his hard thighs beneath her bottom or the sinewy arm sliding around to support her. She was too busy coping with the vibrations pouring out of him to be aware of anything else.

"Luke! What are you doing?"

He scooped her closer, saying, "You're the mind reader. You tell me what's going on."

Desire. A man's longing for a woman, she thought in dazed recognition. His woman. That was what was going on. Waves of pure masculine hunger were rolling over her— as well as deeper, underlying notes of passion, possession, impatience and just a tad of testiness. But the curiosity was gone, she realized. He knew what it was like to kiss her— and for her to respond.

"I've tried to wait, to give you time, but—"

"Give me time?" She blinked up at him. "Luke, we haven't even known each other two weeks."

"A *long* two weeks," he agreed grimly. "I wanted you in my bed the first time I saw you. Touch me, Megan," he muttered, beginning to unravel her braid. "I want to feel your hands on me."

Caught in a whirlwind of emotions, not knowing where his ended and hers began, she started to unbutton his shirt. "Luke, I—"

"I know. You don't think this is smart."

"It's not that."

"You think we're rushing things."

"I'm just—"

"I told you the other night, you can stop me anytime you want." His abrupt words were a direct contrast to the gentle touch of his hands on her hair. He tunneled his fingers through the lush strands, bringing a handful forward over each shoulder, watching it slide down to her waist. "I just want to hold you, to touch you."

"Will you *listen* to me?"

He drew in a sharp breath. "What?"

"I want to feel you, too, and I can't pull your shirt out of your pants."

Luke groaned and shifted her until she was straddling his legs. He leaned forward and pulled at his shirt, tearing it off and tossing it aside. He disposed of hers the same way, following it with her wispy bra.

He settled back, taking in the gentle swell of her breasts, the pebbled nipples peeking through the fire of her hair. He wasn't even aware of the tree bark biting into his back.

"You're beautiful," Megan breathed, stroking his chest and lacing her fingers through the dark mat of crisp hair.

He groaned again at the touch of her slim fingers. "That's my line," he told her. "You're the one who's—" He broke off, sucking in his breath as she tentatively touched his nipples, bringing them to hard, aching nubs.

She hesitated, looking up from the temptation of his chest to meet his dark eyes. Black, she thought. His eyes are black. Not brown, not a bit of both, but pure black. "I'm what?"

"Beautiful. Gorgeous. Sexy." He cupped her bottom with his large hands and slid her closer, until she was pressed against the hard ridge of his arousal.

She opened her mouth to reply just as he pulled her to him. His lips were incredibly soft, smooth and firm, fitting over hers tenderly, completely. Megan forgot what she had intended to say, lost in the sensations of his flesh against hers. She murmured a soft sound as one large hand eased through her hair, cradling her head, holding her at the perfect angle for his lips to brush hers. Again. And again.

His other hand worked down her back, fingers caressing her spine. She nestled closer, making a soft sound when it moved back up, cupping the weight of her breast.

She was surrounded, Megan thought hazily. His thighs flexed beneath her, his hard arm pressed against her back, molding her to his chest. She was surrounded by long muscles and fevered skin. Surrounded by a man whose mind was sending hot and wild messages.

Her hands slipped up and her fingers tightened in his hair, hanging on as one image after another swept through her. Megan shivered and clung to Luke, overwhelmed by sensations—his crisp chest hair tantalizing her sensitive nipples—and an image of the two of them, legs entwined, bodies slick with sweat, in Luke's bed.

Luke abruptly lifted his head. "What's that?" he asked thickly.

"What?" All Megan could hear was the pounding of her blood.

"That." Luke swore, steadily and quietly, desperately battling to control his body. He lifted her off his lap and reached for her clothes. "Here, honey, put them on. We've got company."

Dazed by the sudden change in him, Megan took a ragged breath and stared at his stony face. "Who?"

His eyes bleak with frustration, he said, "Your magician gardener and his sons, I suppose. I forgot he was coming out today to look things over. Hurry, sweetheart, I don't want him catching an eyeful of the wrong thing."

Luke surged to his feet and tugged her up beside him. He looked around to gauge the distance of the truck, then nudged her behind the massive tree and dropped a hard kiss on her upturned lips.

"This is going to take a while," he said grimly, scooping up his shirt and slinging it over his shoulder. "I'll be back as soon as I can. Stay here."

"Why?"

Satisfaction gleamed in his dark eyes. "Because you look too well-kissed, that's why. One look at you would blow any cover story you'd tell him about being out here to work." With another oath, he stalked toward the battered pickup pulling to a stop at the front of the house.

Megan clutched her clothes to her breast and watched him walk away. When she could no longer see him, she sagged against the tree trunk and let out a long, shaky breath.

This is just the beginning.

That evening Megan smoothly swam the length of her pool, kicking off in a racing turn when she reached the end. She had lost count of the laps, but it didn't matter. She would swim until she was numb, she decided. That way she had a chance of exorcising the restless frustration coiled inside her and getting a good night's sleep.

If she did, it would be the first in a long time.

Since she had met Lucas McCall, to be precise.

She had learned a lot about Luke, and everything she'd learned had simply affirmed what she had sensed the first day he had come to the house—that she had every reason to be afraid of him. Yet, when she had told Devin how she felt, she hadn't understood why.

Now she did.

Then, the problem had merely been professional, different approaches to a job. Now, she had to protect herself from a man who wanted her but didn't love her.

Megan kicked off the side of the pool, releasing a little of the tension, relishing the smooth play of muscles as she rhythmically stroked from one end to the other.

Luke was a self-contained man, she reflected, revealing only what he wanted to show. And that was very little—unless he was aroused. Even if it made sense, she reflected as she glided across the pool, it wasn't easy to deal with. Whatever the reason, he was determined to be in control—of himself and everything around him.

He wanted her. He made no secret of the fact. His dark eyes gleamed with a fierce hunger that he didn't even try to hide. It wasn't just her body he was after—he wanted her warmth, her humor, her intelligence, even her anger.

Luke wanted her in every way a man wants a woman—except one. He didn't want her permanently. As far as she could tell, he didn't want *anyone* on a permanent basis.

The scary thing about it was that he seemed to think it was enough.

And it might be, for some women. But not for any raised in the Murphy clan, Megan thought, swimming to the side and pulling herself out of the water.

All of her life, she had been shown in a thousand ways just how much she was loved. As an infant, relatives had clustered around to stroke and pet her. Growing up, there had been any number of family members to share her adolescent joys and disasters. They were still there, and always would be. She had grown accustomed to that kind of support—whether she needed it or not.

Luke was exactly the kind of trouble that she didn't need, Megan told herself as she snatched a towel and rubbed herself briskly. It wasn't that he lacked feelings. On the contrary, he was probably passionate enough for both of them. That had come through loud and clear that afternoon at the plantation. And every time he touched her. Between his psychic emanation and the way he touched her, he could probably burn them both to cinders.

The trouble would begin afterwards—when he left.

And he would.

It might be days, weeks or even months, but he would eventually decide she had come too close, maybe even worked herself into his heart. He'd back away and leave her in splinters of misery.

No intelligent woman would knowingly put herself through that, Megan thought, wrapping the large towel around her like a sarong.

And I'm intelligent.

Only a masochist would get involved with Luke McCall.

And I don't do pain very well.

Looking up at the star-studded sky, she wondered aloud, "So why did I fall in love with him?"

Six

Love?

Megan stared at the stars, her mind turning over the astonishing idea. After a long moment, she turned toward the lanai, automatically pressing her fingertips into the soil of several flowerpots along the way. Satisfied that they were moist enough, she went into the kitchen and looked around, vaguely surprised to find herself there.

In love? With *Luke?*

Shaking her head, she opened the refrigerator and removed a chilled bottle of Riesling, wondering if the cold white wine would clear her head.

Something had to.

She was crazy, she decided calmly. Certifiably nuts. Or had a death wish. Getting any more involved with Luke than she already was would not be a clever move. She knew it, and Devin knew it. The only one who didn't was her mother.

Megan took a sip of wine and contemplated life with her mother. At the moment, it was easier than coping with thoughts of Luke. Mei's talent was not easy to deal with. In fact, it was fair to say that people had been known to avoid her for weeks at a time rather than face her matchmaking look. Which was, of course, precisely the look she had turned on Megan after she'd touched Luke's hand.

The only difference, Megan told herself calmly, slugging down the rest of the wine faster than she'd intended, was that her mother was wrong this time.

Dead wrong.

She and Luke were complete opposites, Megan reminded herself as she returned the bottle to the refrigerator. And despite the old saying, opposites didn't always attract. At least, not for long.

No, she and Luke were simply not long-term material. They were as mismatched as her sister, Liann, and Cody had been. Their tumultuous relationship had once fascinated half the island population...and had ended in marriage nine years ago, she reminded herself glumly. They were still madly in love and now had five-year-old twins.

Not a good example, she decided briskly, shaking her still-damp hair and heading for the living room. With a little time, she'd find a better one.

Just as she entered the room, the doorbell rang.

Megan's heart leapt to her throat and she shot a surprised glance at the oak clock on the wall. Luke? she wondered uneasily.

She didn't want to see him.

Not yet.

Not now.

After what had happened between them this afternoon, she needed time. A year or so would be nice. It might help clear away the confusion, give her time to build a few barriers—like a ten-foot wall and a moat.

No, it wouldn't be Luke. When Mr. Kimura's son had eventually found her by the banyan tree, he'd told her that the two men would probably be busy for hours and that Luke had recommended she take the truck home. He would ride back with the Kimuras. She had agreed, figuring that they both needed time to cool off, that Luke would spend the evening at the hotel.

Besides, it was late, she reminded herself. By now, Luke was undoubtedly in bed, and there was only one other person who would come calling at this time of night.

"Dev?" Her hand was on the doorknob when the bell chimed again with such determination that she didn't need ESP to be certain that it wasn't her brother, after all.

Megan opened the door a crack, knowing who she would find.

She was right.

"Luke! What on earth are you doing here?"

Luke flattened his hand against the door and pushed steadily inward until Megan stepped back and let him in. He closed the door behind him, leaned against it and gazed at her, taking in the midnight-blue towel with a raking glance.

"I'm here because we've got some unfinished business," he said evenly.

"Unfinished . . . ?" The word dwindled away along with her nerve as she felt the determination emanating from him. After a moment, she rallied and tried again, wondering if a little nagging would lighten the charged mood. "Are you out of your mind? It's after midnight!"

"I just left Mr. Kimura."

She shook her head. "I know Al Kimura. He doesn't work this late."

"He was excited about the job," Luke said laconically, pushing away from the door and moving toward her. "I got a guided tour of my own property, a lecture about every tree, and a branch-by-branch description of what would be pruned. Then we went to dinner and he drew pictures of the whole estate on a pile of napkins, just so I wouldn't forget. After that, we drew up a contract for the job—"

"On a napkin?"

"He just happened to have a blank form with him. So we sealed the bargain with a drink, and he brought me home."

"He brought you *here*," she corrected, wondering how quickly she could get him back out the door.

"Whatever." He took another long step in her direction. "You have my truck here."

Suddenly conscious of the fact that she was still wrapped in a towel, Megan hastily sat down and waved him to a chair. "Did he know that?"

"I don't know. I didn't bother telling him." Luke ignored the chair and settled beside her on the sofa. "Does it matter?"

"Mr. Kimura is a friend of the family," she said between clenched teeth, spelling it out for him. "He goes fishing with my dad all the time. He landscaped my yard, so he knows that I live here."

Luke grinned down at her, enjoying her temper. "You're right. He does. When I told him to drop me off at your place, he drove right to it."

Megan heaved an exasperated sigh. "Subtle, McCall. Real subtle."

"What's the problem?"

"The problem," she said testily, "is the local grapevine. It's incredible. By tomorrow afternoon, everyone who knows either one of us will be discussing the fact that he brought you here in the middle of the damn night! I don't like having everyone looking at me and speculating."

"It's no one else's business," he said evenly. "If any of them have any questions, refer them to me. Besides," he added in a more reasonable tone, "I've spent the last four days here. And the evenings. And almost everyone in your family has either dropped by while I was here or telephoned. I don't see the difference."

Megan looked at him and shook her head. He was so *dense.* "The difference is that you were here during the day and we were *working.* Now—"

"Ah. The duck theory."

She shot him a distracted frown. "The what?"

"If it looks like a duck and quacks like a duck and waddles like a duck, it must be a duck. Right?"

"I suppose."

"But now it doesn't look like a duck anymore. It looks like—"

"Something that it isn't. Up to now, we were—"

"—working," he finished for her. "But this afternoon changed everything."

"No, it didn't." She shook her head, infuriated by his cool assurance. Not only was he dense, he was stubborn. As well as persistent. And if she gave an inch, he'd take two miles, and before she knew it he'd be moving in with her. Her heart lurched in her chest at the thought, and she said a little shakily, "This afternoon was a . . . mistake."

Luke's eyes narrowed. "Like hell it was. You knew it was coming as well as I did. I'd say it was not only inevitable, it was long overdue."

Megan shook her head, sending strands of damp hair tumbling over her shoulders. In desperation, she looked straight at him and lied through her teeth. "Luke, it was just one of those things that happen, probably because we've been together so much. Just a case of propinquity," she said carelessly. "Nothing to get excited about."

Luke's heart thumped with a feeling that was close to panic. She was lying—she had to be. She wanted him as much as he wanted her. She had been fire in his arms, touching him, clinging to him, making those soft sweet sounds deep in her throat when he'd kissed her.

But now she'd had time to cool down, to think. To compare him to other men—men who used silky voices and soft words to seduce a woman. To men who spoke of love.

Fury swept through him, and he wanted to pick her up and shake her. Propinquity, hell. She was going to toss away the best thing that had ever happened to him because she was too stubborn to admit the truth. She was too—

Luke stopped and drew in a deep breath while he took a good look at her—at the way she had scooted back into the corner of the couch, at her wide blue eyes.

Scared.

She was scared.

Luke gazed at her, dumbfounded. She was scared of him. He blinked, trying to take it in. She...was...afraid. Of him. Outrage mingled with pure terror until his mind flashed back to that afternoon at the plantation. She had trembled in his arms, but it hadn't been fear.

Hell no, it hadn't. She had been ripping off his shirt with an urgency that equaled his. Her fingers had been shaking when she'd kneaded his chest. Her frustration had matched his own when Kimura's truck had come down the dirt road.

No, he thought exultantly, it wasn't *of* him. She was scared right out of her cute little sarong by what was happening between them, what she was feeling *for* him.

Relief swept through him, and he wanted to scoop her up and tell her there was no reason to worry. He almost did until common sense forced him to slow down. She wasn't going to believe a word he said. He was the reason she'd gone crazy this afternoon, and she wouldn't trust him to walk her across the street. Especially if she had to touch him.

No, talk wasn't going to cut it. The only thing she'd listen to was her own body—and it was obviously telling her to keep her distance.

Luke extended one hand and wound a lock of her hair around his finger. Ignoring her nervous blink, he smoothed it with his thumb while he concentrated on keeping his voice casual.

"So today was just something that happened."

"Mmm-hmm."

"Propinquity?"

Megan nodded energetically, a look of such relief crossing her face he almost laughed. "Trust me," she assured him. "That's all it was."

"Nothing to get excited about?"

Her eyes narrowed at his mild tone, wariness suddenly replacing relief. "Right."

Luke looked down at the fiery hair twined around his finger, biting back a smile as she shifted gears. Her uneasiness was palpable. She was as tense as a cat, ready to leap if he so much as blinked his eyes. And, by God, her instincts were right on target, because he had waited as long as he intended to wait. Tonight was the night. But first, he had to bring the wary little kitten out of the corner. Then he had to get her to sheathe her claws and touch him.

Luke contemplated the hand he had tangled in her tousled hair. That was the key, he brooded—touching. When she put her hands on him—however casually—he burned. He wanted to toss her over his shoulder and head for the nearest bed.

He didn't know exactly what happened to Megan when they touched, but the way her clear eyes clouded over, the reaction was potent. He recalled how she edged away if he got too close, how she avoided touching him when she could and wondered if this psychic thing put a spin on it for her, made it even stronger. He'd lay odds that it did.

He hoped to hell it did.

Megan shook her head, detaching her hair from his fingers, and jumped to her feet, not really surprised when he followed her. She reached for her tote bag and fumbled until she found what she was looking for.

"Here are the keys," she said, turning back to him. "I thought— What are you *doing?*"

Luke calmly finished unbuttoning his shirt. "While Mr. Kimura and I were playing in the jungle, I got a thorn stuck in my chest. I thought the family healer might want to take a look." He didn't bother telling her that the sticker had been removed hours ago.

"Let me see," Megan said, moving closer and tilting her head to look. "It's still red. Did you get it all out?"

"I guess."

"You don't guess about things like that," she lectured absently, peering at the inflamed area. "Even a particle could cause an infection."

She delicately stroked the small welt, testing it with the tip of her finger. "It's a little swollen." She frowned, then placed her palm on the spot, checking to see if it was feverish.

It was. Or at least it was hot.

But so was the rest of him. Heat radiated from his body in waves. Megan froze when his heartbeat increased perceptibly, the rhythm matching her own pounding pulse.

"That's it, honey," Luke said quietly. "Touch me."
Slowly he reached up, covering her small hand with his,
holding it in place.

Instinctively, Megan attempted to pull away, but Luke
tightened his grip—not enough to hurt, just enough to keep
her where she was.

Megan stilled. It was too late. It had been too late the instant he'd touched her. Sensations brushed through her,
cautiously at first, then intensifying with every heartbeat.
Desire . . . hunger . . . and overwhelming need. Her own feelings rose to meet and match his. Her thoughts scattered
when he covered her mouth in a hard kiss.

A long moment later she looked at him with dazed eyes
and gave it one last shot. "Luke," she whispered, "we
should stop. Right now."

"No way, honey. Not this time."

Megan saw her reflection in his black eyes. It didn't take
a psychic to know what he saw—a woman whose soothing
touch had become a gentle kneading action, a woman who
rubbed against him like a cat. A woman ready for love.

"You're right," she said, reaching up for another one of
his drugging kisses. "Not this time."

A slow, very feminine smile lit her face when he gave a
blink of surprise that quickly turned to relief.

"Ah, sweetheart, I've waited so damn long to hear that."
He gave her a searching glance and his arms tightened
around her even as he asked, "Are you sure?"

She smiled. "Yes." And she was. After all her doubts, all
her arguments, it boiled down to one thing—she loved him.
This man. God knew he could turn her life upside down
without even trying, but while he was doing it she knew he
would hold her heart safely in his large hands.

Luke grinned as he swung her up in his arms and headed
for the stairs.

"Luke!" Her blue eyes laughed up at him. "The door."

"I locked it when I came in."

She waved a hand around the room. "The lights are on."

"I'll pay the damn bill. I'm not putting you down until we're in your room."

"Well, you don't have to carry me. I won't run away." And she wouldn't, now that she had made up her mind.

"Quit wiggling." He heard her reassurance beneath the teasing words and felt her body melting against his, but he still wasn't taking any chances. Stepping through the bedroom doorway, he paused near the light switch. When Megan reached out to touch it, a small corner lamp sent a soft glow around the room.

He kept her in his arms while he looked around the room, thinking as he had the first day he saw it that it was a perfect reflection of Megan. Utterly feminine, enchanting without being fussy. A large, brass bedstead—probably an antique—white wicker lounge chairs, dark green carpeting and pale yellow walls. The curtains were white and sheer, while the bedspread and pillows were a riot of vivid colors.

It was an inviting room.

A seductive room.

Megan touched his chin. "Why the frown?"

"I was wondering how many—"

Her hand slid to his mouth, cutting off the words. "You're the first man I've invited to my room."

Luke kissed her hand and eased her down, deliberately letting her slide the length of his hard body. When she was standing in the circle of his arms, he said bluntly, "That brings up another point. I don't want to hurt you. Are you a vir—"

Megan stood on tiptoe and brushed her lips against his. "No, but thank you for asking." Flattening her hands on his chest, she furrowed her fingers in the crisp dark hair. "Are the preliminaries over now?" she asked politely.

A groan cut off Luke's laugh when she touched her thumbs to his nipples. His answer was a growl and a string of hot kisses that went from her temple to her shoulder. She arched reflexively against him, murmuring, her lips moving against his throat.

"Why are you wearing a damp towel?" he muttered.

"Because I was swimming."

Luke dropped a hard deep kiss on her lips, softening it as she flung her arms around his neck. With his eyes closed, he caught a faint whiff of chlorine and he tasted wine. Using both hands, he traced the satiny skin above the towel until he found the edge tucked beneath the fabric. He tugged at it, letting the towel fall to the floor.

When he pulled her closer, one hand tracing the length of her elegant spine—he almost exploded. She was naked.

Megan felt his jolt of surprise and the convulsive movement of his arousal. She tilted her head back and grinned up at him. "I guess I forgot to tell you. I don't wear a suit when I swim alone."

Her eyes widened and she made a bereft sound when he dropped his hands and took a step back.

"Don't move," he muttered. "Just stay still for a minute. You're so beautiful, honey. I want to see you."

Luke's searing gaze was as potent as a touch. It left her shaky—her body reacting as if he were stroking her with his long fingers—and surprisingly unselfconscious. She gloried in the fact that she could bring such a look of dark appreciation to his eyes—and the hungry, obvious arousal to his hard body.

His gaze started at the top of her head, at the tumbled redgold hair that coiled around her like a living frame. Her lips dried and her breath shortened when his eyes dropped to her mouth. When it went even lower, her breasts tingled and her nipples beaded into hot nubs of sensation. She instinctively lifted her hands in an ageless gesture of feminine concealment, stopping when he took one hand and brought it to his lips.

"No. Don't." He kissed her palm and slowly returned her hand. "Don't hide from me."

Megan shivered, knowing her body was betraying her need, tightening as his gaze traveled even lower. When it stopped at the russet hair beneath the gentle swell of her belly, shafts of hot tension worked from her nipples to her loins and she broke. Flinging herself at him, her shaky hands slid up his hard chest, stopping at his shoulders and tugging at his shirt.

"Sweetheart, wait. Wait a second. We're getting all tangled up in it." He swore in frustration. When her blue eyes questioned him, he groaned and dropped a torrid kiss on her lips. With only a breath separating them, he said breathlessly, "I can do it quicker."

He held her close with one arm, glorying in the restless movements of her body, while he pulled off his shirt and tore off the bedspread, tossing them both aside. After he drew back the sheet he swung her up in his arms and dropped her gently in the center of the big bed.

"Be right there," he promised.

He was right, Megan decided, turning her head to watch him with fascinated eyes. He could do it quicker. It was a much more efficient arrangement. But the sight of his muscular, hairy chest and hard belly set off a reaction that had nothing to do with practicality.

He didn't look away from her as he tugged off his shoes and socks. A tremor went through Megan at the heat of his gaze and her breath caught when his hands moved to his waist, the soft rasp of his zipper sounding loud in the stillness of the room.

Luke removed several packets from his back pocket, then hooked his thumbs in the waistband of his jeans, pushing them down, removing his cotton briefs at the same time. He stepped out of them and stalked closer to the bed.

Megan turned to face him, anticipation mingling with sudden uneasiness. Luke was beautiful and she had an indecent urge to run her hands all over him, gliding over crisp hair and taut muscles. He was also a very large man—tall, broad-shouldered and muscular—and she wasn't sure how he managed it, but somehow he looked even bigger without clothes.

And—she assessed the most salient point with a quick glance—he was magnificently aroused.

Maybe she had been a bit hasty, she reflected edgily, scooting toward the edge of the bed when he eased down beside her. After all, this was a big step to take. A *very* big step, and—

"Whoa," he said gently, wrapping his long arm around her waist and drawing her back to him. "Don't run away. I just got here."

Megan watched him with widening eyes as he propped himself on a forearm and looked down at her, his shoulders blocking out most of the lamplight. "Uh, Luke—"

"Hmm?"

"I was just thinking."

"Yeah?" The one word brimmed with resigned amusement.

"Maybe we miscalculated a bit here."

He leaned down to drop a light kiss on her nose. "Honey, are you a little nervous about this?"

"Of course not!" she said quickly. Too quickly. She was a *lot* nervous. "I just thought that maybe—" Her words stopped with a gasp when his hand brushed her aching breast.

"Maybe what?"

She shrugged and realized belatedly that the movement had just slid her breast into his cupped hand. "I don't know," she said vaguely, dealing with the aftermath of shock from her erect nipple.

His thumb grazed over the tight bud again. "Are you really not a virgin?"

"I told you I wasn't," she muttered, moving restlessly beneath the stroking fingers. "But that doesn't mean I make a *habit* of this, you know."

Luke reluctantly quit what he was doing and cupped her chin with his fingers. "Megan, how many times have you made—" He swore softly, stopped and started again. "How many times have you slept with a man?"

She looked at him, outraged. "That's absolutely none of your business! Am I asking you for—"

He cut her off by the simple expedient of putting his hand over her mouth. "Ordinarily, you'd be right," he said grimly. "But I think we have an exception to the rule here. I don't want you hurt because I've made a wrong assumption." When she stared up at him with mutinous eyes, he said again, "How many times?"

She opened her mouth, but her eyes gave her away. He moved his fingers just before her teeth snapped, missing him by a breath.

"How many?"

Megan glared at him, knowing he'd keep repeating the question all night—or at least until he got an answer. "Four," she said sulkily.

Luke stared at his twenty-six-year-old legend in disbelief. "Four?"

"I think."

"You think?"

"Well," she said thoughtfully, willing to explain now that the worst was over, "they weren't exactly what you'd call momentous occasions. Some of them were highly forgettable, so I'm not really sure."

"Not really sure," he repeated in an expressionless voice. "And how long has it been since the last forgettable occasion?"

"Approximately?"

Luke sighed. "Yeah, that'll do. Give or take a few months." She was silent for so long his nerves stretched to the breaking point. His virginal non-virgin was driving him crazy. He wondered if she had any idea how near he was to exploding. He hoped to hell not. She didn't need an early starter and fast finisher to add to her collection.

"Two years."

Luke blinked, switching slowly from his thoughts to her statement. "What?"

"Two years," she repeated. "More or less."

When he thought he had himself in hand, Luke said, "Two years. Two *years?*"

"I've been busy," she said defensively. "Building a business takes a lot of time. Besides," she muttered when he just continued to stare at her, "it seemed like a lot of fuss about nothing. It just wasn't worth the trouble."

She glared up at him as she put her hand on his shoulder and shoved. It was like trying to move a boulder, she decided, giving up. "If that bothers you," she began belligerently, "we can just forget—"

This time it was his mouth that stopped her words. A mouth that settled on hers as if it were made just for that purpose. A mouth that soothed and promised and coaxed until she parted her lips for him and melted against him, sliding her hands into his hair, holding him close.

She responded to his touch the same way, as if she had been created for the hands that glided over her, pausing here to graze acutely sensitive flesh, stopping there for a longer communion.

When he came up for air, Luke sounded as if he'd been running. Looking down at her bemused face, he asked, "Are you still nervous?"

Megan touched his face lightly, tracing one dark brow with her fingertip. "What?"

"That's what I thought." He brushed her shoulder with his lips, smiling against her silky skin when she shivered. "You're so beautiful."

She shook her head. "No, I'm just your common variety, half Hawaiian, half Irish offshoot. Now, if you want to talk about drop-dead gorgeous, take a look at my sister, Liann. She's the—"

Luke shook his head. "You're as much beauty as I can handle." He looked into her doubting eyes and vowed that by morning Megan would not only consider herself beautiful, she'd have a night and a man that she would never forget. He intended to impress her body with his touch so she would never even think of another man.

He grazed her beaded breasts with his tongue, lingering to savor the sweetness, until she gasped.

"Luke!"

"Mmm?"

"That feels so..."

"What?"

She sighed. "Good."

"I know."

He shifted his weight, his warm breath caressing the soft swell of her belly. When she sighed again, this time shakily, he moved lower.

Megan stilled, hardly breathing as ineffable tension drew her body taut. Her breath came in shallow gasps.

"Luke?"

"I'm not going anywhere." His lips touched her inner thigh.

"I didn't know..."

"Shh."

Her hips lifted in a small, uncontrollable movement, an ageless, involuntary signal of approval, acceptance. It also triggered a small flare of panic. "Luke, I don't think I can—"

"Yes, you can, sweetheart. Believe me, you can." His hands tightened on her hips, then eased, his fingers stroking, soothing until she relaxed.

It was good that one of them could, he thought grimly. The flexing of her supple body was so incredibly arousing, Luke closed his eyes and began counting backward. He was not about to lose control before Megan achieved at his hands the one thing no other man had given her.

He wanted her turning to fire in his hands, twisting and burning in his arms. Making those soft sounds in her throat, moaning, clinging to him, calling his name in a breathless voice. And if it took all night—

"Oh! Luke." She clutched at his hair. "No more."

"Hmm?"

"I... mean it."

He smiled.

"You're... driving... me... crazy."

"Good. That's the way I want you. Out of control. Crazy. For me. About me. All over me."

It didn't take all night. The next instant she cried out in a voice drugged with desire. "Luke. *Now.* I need you."

He slid up, grabbing and tearing open a packet. "Do you *want* me?" He braced his forearms on either side of her head, looking down into dazed blue eyes.

Her hips lifted against him in silent urgency.

"Now?" He tested himself against her.

"Yesss." Megan's legs wrapped around him, holding him close as she trembled with unfamiliar passion. *"Now."* Her voice broke and she slid her arms around his neck, holding on for dear life.

He covered her mouth with his and sheathed himself in her softness.

Megan convulsed around him, shimmering, burning, shuddering with a pleasure so fierce it bordered on pain. Only when her breath began to steady did Luke give in to his own shattering release.

Much later, with Megan lying in his arms, one slim leg tucked between his, he tightened his arm around her. "Are you okay?"

She grinned sleepily. "I'm marvelous."

"You're right about that."

"Luke?"

"Hmm?"

"That was..."

Luke tensed. "Was what?"

"So incredible," she said in wonder. "Surely it doesn't happen that way very often."

He relaxed, realizing just how tightly drawn he'd been. Grinning down at her, he said, "You'll find out. Later."

Megan blinked. "Later?"

"Later." He dropped a kiss on her shoulder. "I told you this was just the beginning."

Seven

"**G**ood morning."

"Mmpff."

"You're right," Luke said, his voice warm with amusement—as well as blatant masculine satisfaction. "It's going to be another beautiful day in paradise."

"Oh, God," Megan moaned, stubbornly keeping her eyes closed. "I spent the night with a man who wakes up giving weather reports."

And what a night, she thought hazily, memories nudging her toward awareness faster than she normally made the transition. It had not been restful but it had been one she would remember for the rest of her life.

"I take it we're not a person who, uh, starts the day at full speed?" His voice rumbled beneath her ear.

"Bingo," Megan muttered, making a supreme effort to be coherent. "We're not a person who talks or even opens our eyes for the first ten or fifteen minutes. We do not leap out of bed and make coffee or breakfast.''

"Okay with me," he said with disgusting cheerfulness. "I'm just fine right here."

Here, Megan reflected, was holding her, his naked body plastered to hers from cheek to toes.

Waking up in a man's arms was an . . . interesting experience, she decided groggily. Especially if the arms belonged to Luke.

As always, Luke seemed to have things under control. She was stretched out on top of him, using him for both bed and pillow. One of his large hands was at her waist while the other softly kneaded her bottom. All things considered, she thought drowsily, there were worse ways to wake up.

And with that thought, she promptly went back to sleep.

Luke gritted his teeth as she moved, sliding one leg between his, her belly brushing his hardening flesh. It was torture, but a torture he'd gladly endure—as long as she stayed right where she was.

A minute later he was wondering about the limit of both his endurance and sanity as Megan stirred again, shifting her hips restlessly in sinuous movements that drove him wild. As if drawn by a magnet, her pelvis sought the heat of his, settling against him with a gentle thrust.

If she hadn't been asleep, he would have taken her right then. But she was. She was also not ready for another bout of uninhibited sex. By her own accounting, it had been two years—more or less—and she was bound to be—

"Hot," Megan said clearly.

"As hell," he agreed through clenched teeth.

She mumbled something dark and incomprehensible into his chest, then nuzzled her cheek against the mat of dark hair that covered it.

Luke sucked in his breath, knowing he was about ten seconds away from exploding. He rolled to his side, taking Megan with him, easing her down on the mattress, watching her glorious hair cover the pillow like a bright banner. The sheet had been kicked off during the night and she lay there, soft and feminine, sleek and naked.

She wouldn't be embarrassed to find herself that way, he decided after debating about searching for the sheet. Megan seemed comfortable with her body, clothed or not. Which suited him just fine. He didn't want her covered a second sooner than she had to be.

Then he knew he was going to find out if he was right. She opened her eyes, looking straight into his.

"Hi," she said softly, reaching up to test his bristly chin with her thumb. Her hand moved farther up, lacing through dark rumpled hair that fell over his brow. "You look like a pirate." A dashing, gorgeous, sexy pirate.

He grinned, waiting. "Are you awake now?"

"Almost." Her blue gaze drifted first down his body, then her own. A small, satisfied smile curved her lips. "Nice."

"Very."

Megan turned on her side and backed into him, spoon fashion. Reaching for his hand, she brought it up to cover her breast, keeping her hand on his, holding it there.

Luke felt sweat break out on his forehead and began counting backward from a hundred. He wanted to hold her every bit as much as she wanted to be held, but he wanted to do a hell of a lot more, and she had already been pushed to the limit.

He knew he was right a minute later when she lifted her arms in a stretch that thrust her breast deeper into his palm—and stopped, wincing.

Luke swore softly and dropped a kiss on her shoulder. "Sore?"

She nodded. "A little."

"Sweetheart, I'm sorry. I should have known better. I should have stopped—"

Megan turned and put her fingers over his mouth. "You didn't do anything I didn't want you to do." She grinned up at him. "In fact, I seem to remember waking you up the last time."

He kissed her fingers. "Even so, I should—"

"Wrong." She shook her head serenely. "It wasn't your responsibility. I knew how I felt and I knew what I wanted. You." She grinned again. "And I had you, didn't I?"

He squeezed her breast gently. "Yeah, you sure did. And you'll have me again if I don't get out of here."

"Luke?" Megan clutched his hand as he started to move, pressing it against her.

He sighed sharply and lowered his head. The kiss lasted a long time, until Megan moaned and brushed her hand over his hard body.

"No." He lifted his head after another quick kiss. "Sweetheart, that's the nicest invitation I've ever had, but I'm not going to hurt you. It can wait. Neither one of us is going anywhere."

He rolled off the bed and scooped up the sheet, shaking it and letting it drift down to cover her. "What I *am* going to do is take a shower while you stay here, then go down and start breakfast. Meet me in the kitchen when you're ready."

Nibbling on a bit of papaya, Megan said thoughtfully, "I think you should have a name for each of the plantations. Your advertising would list them all as McCall's, of course, but feature each one by name. It has a certain cachet, don't you think?"

"Real class," he agreed amiably, taking a swallow of coffee, aware that he was feeling better than he had in a long, long time. Megan had that effect on him. She had several other unique and very distinct effects on him, he silently admitted, recalling how she had looked before he'd dropped the sheet on her. It was his cross to bear that most of them ended the same way, with his body heavy and hard.

"And I think you should have a painting done of the original house."

"Why?" Luke watched her over the rim of his cup. She was wide-awake now, practically vibrating with ideas and energy.

"To hang in the entryway of the new one." Her enthusiasm for the idea mounting, she added, "It should have a rainbow in it. No, it *has* to have one—ending at the roof. In fact, the painting should be called 'Rainbow's End.'"

"Why?" Luke asked again, smiling as excitement turned her eyes aquamarine.

"I'm getting to that."

"Megan—"

She waved him to silence with her fork, a piece of papaya waving precariously at the end. "I learned the most wonderful stuff about the original owners when I was there yesterday, Luke. If I hadn't been distracted—" her grin forgave him for the interruption "—I would have told you about it on the way home. Anyway, those people had a real old-fashioned romance."

"Honey—"

Her eyes sparkled at the thought. "The man who built the house was head over heels in love with his new bride. He sawed, hammered and plastered his feelings into every square inch of the place. He planted the trees on land that could have been used more practically simply because she loved them."

Luke's smile faded and he carefully replaced his cup on the table, trying to deal with the surge of emotion that burned his insides. He wasn't jealous, he told himself. He had never been jealous in his life. It was a stupid emotion, one that a smart man wouldn't—

"—and he got the most up-to-date linoleum for her kitchen."

Hell, yes, he was jealous. After last night, he had good reason to be. He had taken the red-haired legend to places and heights she had never even dreamed of, and he figured he had exclusive rights to her attention. Less than an hour ago she had been hot and excited in his arms, and now there was envy and longing in her eyes when she talked about another man.

His eyes narrowed in outrage even while he knew he was being unreasonable. But, damn it, if she wanted to get dewy-eyed over a man, it should be him, the one who made her body shimmer and burn. It didn't soothe him at all to hear the other man had been crazy about his wife and dead for fifty years. It was the principle of the thing—Megan belonged to him.

"And," she ended triumphantly, "he named the plantation Rainbow's End because it held everything in the world that was precious to him." She gave a pensive sigh, then popped the last bite of papaya in her mouth. "Isn't that a wonderful story?"

"Yeah," he said abruptly. "A great story. But that's all it is, Megan. Just a story."

"What do you mean?" Dreamily considering the century-old drama, she tilted her head and looked at him, smiling, her fork still poised in midair.

The adrenaline pouring through his body made his voice harsher than he'd intended. "I mean that it's not true, Megan. I'll grant you this—you have one hell of an imagination. You walk into these old places and get these ideas and concoct—"

"You think I made it all up?"

Luke swore when he saw the stricken look in her eyes. She looked like she had aged ten years in the blink of an eye. "I think," he said carefully, "that your imagination takes you to places that haven't really existed. They're not real."

Megan's smile was brittle. "What you're saying is that I need a reality check?"

"Damn it! I didn't say that." Luke reached across the table for her hand—a hand that disappeared before he got close.

"Let me tell you something about reality, Luke." A shadow crossed her face, bleaching it of all animation and joy. "I spend a lot of time there. It's a place where nobody believes I experience these things in old houses. That is, if I bother to tell them. The only ones who do are the people I grew up with. Only my family. I learned that a long time ago."

She picked up her cup and looked down into the steaming coffee. "You've probably heard I have a reputation for being independent, for doing things my own way. That's why. I'd never told anyone how I work until you practically made it a condition of the job."

Until you.

Luke winced. He had insisted that she tell him, all right, and now that she had he didn't believe her. What was worse, he didn't have the sense to conceal his growing skepticism. He couldn't have hurt her more if he'd slapped her across the face with the flat of his hand.

"Honey, I didn't mean—"

She raised a hand, stopping him. "I knew the risk of telling people, Luke. Once I got older, I just never thought it was a risk worth taking. Until now." She gave a small, negligent shrug that didn't mask the pain in her eyes. "Well, we live and learn, don't we?"

"Megan," he began desperately, fear beginning to run deep within him. "I didn't mean to hurt you. I only meant that—"

"Luke, how would you describe me?"

He blinked, thrown by the quiet question. "What?"

"If you wanted someone to know me, what would you tell them?"

"Hell, I don't know." He gave an impatient sigh. "That you're beautiful, sexy, warm, impulsive, funny—"

"And a liar?"

Infuriated, he stared at her. "No. Damn it, Megan, I would never say that about you."

"You already have."

The quiet words had a finality that shook Luke to his soul. The whole thing had happened too quickly for him to assimilate. One minute they were lovers, sharing memories and a meal. The next, she had shut him out of her life.

"Look, sweetheart—" *Think, you idiot. Say something to take the devastation out of her eyes.* "I only meant to say—"

"What you believed," she said gently. "It's okay, Luke. Maybe I was expecting the impossible."

"Honey—"

She shook her head. "No. It's not going to work."

"What isn't?" he challenged aggressively, trying to cover the coldness seeping through him.

"Us." She made a vague gesture that included the two of them. "I should have known, because it's happened before. I don't have any control over this thing, Luke, and for better or worse, I see and know things that other people don't. Things from another time. Some of them I've actually been able to document at a later date."

Luke surged out of his chair, barely controlled violence in his dark eyes. "What exactly are you telling me, Megan? I want it in words of one syllable so there's no misunderstanding.''

"All right.'' She took a quick breath. "I don't want to see you again.''

She was courageous, his legend. She wasn't nearly as calm as she pretended to be, but her steady blue gaze practically nailed him to the wall.

"That's going to be a good trick. We have one hell of a job ahead of us for the next year.''

"Other than for the job,'' she amended. "That is, if you still want me to do it.''

He ignored the question, zeroing in on the most vital point. "That's it?'' he said in disbelief. "You're kicking me out because I said something about what you do?''

Hurt, anger and incomprehension poured from him in a stream of pain, battering at Megan until she could barely breathe. She clung to her coffee cup until her knuckles whitened.

"That's the point, Luke. It's not just something I do. It's what I *am*. I know it's hard to believe and even harder to accept, but it's a core part of me. I'm a person with psychic ability, and it makes me different from other people.''

"For God's sake, honey—''

She shook her head. "Let me finish. It's not something I can put aside or pretend not to have. I wouldn't do it even if I could. And...'' She came to a stop, looking at him uncertainly.

"And what?''

"And any man who wants me has to accept that part of me,'' she finished with a rush.

"What the hell do you mean, *any* man?'' he said through clenched teeth. "There's only one. Me. So what are you saying? All I have to do is accept it? Fine. I accept it.''

She was saying goodbye. Luke gazed at her, his eyes narrowed to black slits, refusing to believe what was happening. But one look at her tormented eyes and stiff spine told him all he needed to know—that his legend was also part Amazon, as proud as she was valiant. She would hold back the tears threatening to fall and she would ignore the tremor in her voice—while she broke both their hearts.

Eyes reflecting his pain, Megan shook her head again. "You have to *believe*," she said softly. "I can't live with any less than that."

She gathered the dishes and took them to the sink, busying herself with rinsing and stacking them. With her back to him, she said tightly, "If you want to look for someone else to do the houses, I'll understand."

"You'll understand," he repeated in a voice laced with frustration and fury. "That's a damn sight more than I do. I don't understand any of this. Last night you were in my arms, as hot and wild as running lava, sliding over me like silk, taking me in—"

"Don't!"

"—side you, burning me up with—"

His pain was like a wild thing in the room, cutting off her breath. Megan spun around, bracing herself against the counter. "Luke, stop it!"

He stopped, forgetting what he was saying when he saw the tears glittering on her cheeks. He started to speak, but she was already talking, disjointed words tumbling out, her voice trembling with the need to heal, to make him understand.

"I should have known. It wouldn't work. It never has. Those four times I told you about? The forgettable ones? It wasn't just uninspired sex. They knew...somehow...that I was different. They got scared and left."

She wiped away the tears with her fingers. "It's not your fault, Luke. It's okay. I understand. Last night was beautiful and wonderful. Electrifying. Everything I ever dreamed it could be. It's just that I need . . ."

"What?" Shaken by her words, as well as her tears, his voice gentled. He didn't trust himself to touch her so he slid his hands in his back pockets and tried to listen. "What do you need?"

Megan swallowed painfully. "To be understood. And accepted. Just as I am. For what I am." She turned to look out the window to the lanai.

Staring blindly at the leaves quivering in the breeze, she said, "I can give you some recommendations if you want someone else to do the work."

"No."

She shivered at the terse word. "Then . . . I'll go on as we planned. Day after tomorrow I'll be at the plantation to work with the man you hired. We'll go through the place carefully and I'll send you a written report. It should only take a week or so."

"Fine."

Luke turned and stalked out the door, pausing to grab the keys to the truck. He half turned to go back but stopped as if he had run into a glass wall when he heard the broken sounds of Megan weeping. Swearing savagely, he stalked out the front door and closed it behind him.

He had just reached the four by four when a blue pickup pulled to a stop behind it, spewing gravel and dirt and raising a cloud of dust. Devin leapt out, heading for the house.

"I see you didn't listen to my warning."

Luke stiffened, instinctively reacting to the rage in the icy blue eyes. He unclenched his fist, figuring Megan would take a dim view of having her brother's nose broken. Instead, he raised his arm, blocking the way to the front porch.

"Don't go in there."

Devin stopped just short of Luke's arm, his eyes narrowing at the command. It was softly uttered, but nevertheless a command. "My sister's in there."

"So is the woman I spent the night with." Luke watched as anger flared in the blue eyes and was immediately controlled. "I don't want you to bother her."

"She's crying," Devin said flatly.

Luke drew in a breath of pure exasperation, bewilderment running a close second. Megan had not been reaching for a phone when he left, and even if she had, Devin couldn't have gotten here so soon.

"What the hell is it with you people? You send messages by conch shells or something?"

The tension in Devin eased fractionally at the frustration in both the question and the man before him. He gave an enigmatic shrug. "Something like that. If Megan hasn't explained, I'll be damned if I will." His eyes darkened and he said almost conversationally, "You know, I'd really like the chance to take you apart."

"Yeah." Luke heaved a sharp sigh. "Me, too. But I'm trying to make points with the lady inside, and I don't think beating her brother to a pulp is the way to go about it."

"She's crying," Devin said again, less aggressively this time.

"Hell, I know it. I *caused* it."

"And you're just walking out?"

"I got kicked out."

"Did you hurt her?" Devin was sounding dangerous again.

Luke tamped down his temper, reminding himself that Megan was lucky to have such a fierce watchdog. Too many women were without protection of any kind.

He nodded. "Through sheer stupidity." The admission wasn't easy, but he figured her brother deserved it. "And not physically. I shouldn't even have to say it, but just for the record, I will. I would never deliberately hurt her."

Devin's gaze was speculative as he studied Luke's ravaged face. Finally, the tension left him and he said almost sympathetically, "So what are you going to do?"

"I don't know. Yet. But I'm working on it."

"Do you need help?"

Luke's dark brows rose. "Is that an offer?"

"I don't know. Yet."

"While you're thinking about it, there is something you can do. Stay away from Megan. The last thing I need is her favorite brother telling her what a bastard I am."

Devin's smile was the same flash of brilliance as his sister's. "I don't tell her everything I know."

Later, the memory of that smile haunted him as he paced through the penthouse. Megan had gifted him with it so many times during the past week he had become addicted to it. He needed it as much as he needed air and water. As much as he needed her soft touches and laughter.

As much as he needed *her.*

And, damn it, he had given her more of himself than he had given any woman. For that matter, anyone. He had given more than he knew he had to give.

What the hell did she want from him?

His soul?

He scowled at the high-tech telephone on his desk and was briefly tempted. Since Megan was the first listing on automatic dial, he only had to punch one button and he'd hear her voice.

Yeah, he'd hear it all right—full of tears. Tears he had caused. Then, as soon as she knew who was at the other end, she'd hang up. Not the best idea he'd ever had.

Luke thumbed through his leather-bound telephone book, noting absently that other than Megan's, the listings were all business. Well, he thought dryly, why not? Business was one of the things he did right. Once you knew how to initiate a deal and pace it, there were very few surprises.

Pacing was a key element in any transaction. You didn't let it drag and you sure as hell didn't rush it. Once started, all you generally needed was a little . . .

Patience.

He stared blindly down at the book, a grim twist to his mouth. Patience. The one thing he had completely overlooked in his dealings with Megan. From the minute she had walked into his office with her drawings he had deliberately kept her off balance.

Rushed her.

And now he had to start all over again.

Forty-five hours later, at six in the morning, Luke turned the truck down the rutted road to the plantation. It was early, but he wanted to beat the heat. He also wanted to be there before Megan arrived. Where she was concerned, he needed every advantage he could get.

He made the turn to the house, and with a twist of his wrist cut the motor, quietly pulling in beside an unfamiliar truck. After making a note of the license number, he opened the door and slid down, leaving it ajar. If there was a problem, there was no sense in advertising his arrival.

Using the cover of the trees, he quartered the area around the house. There was probably a reasonable explanation for the truck's presence, he assured himself, but with Megan due in the next few minutes he wasn't taking any chances.

It was hardly the place to expect trouble, he reflected, checking the front porch. It looked like something out of a travelogue—the perfume of flowers filling the air, birds singing their hearts out, trees dipping their leaves in time to the breeze and the sun shining on it all. He was headed around the side, telling himself that he was on a fool's errand, when he heard a noise behind the house, back by the crumpled foundations of the old bungalows.

Just as he got to the corner, Megan—a blur of yellow and white in tank top, shorts and sneakers, her loose hair flying behind her like streamers of red silk—burst out of the tangle of trees, running as if her life depended on her speed.

And it just might, Luke decided grimly, because right on her heels was a man who looked determined to take her down. Tall, he was twice her weight, but still moving fast.

Although she didn't see him, Megan was running straight for Luke, her long legs eating up the distance, bringing her pursuer right along with her.

"Come to papa," Luke murmured, encouraging her from the shadow of the house. His rage mounted as they drew closer and he got a clearer look at the man. Really not much more than a kid, he estimated. Eighteen, maybe nineteen. Probably on a hormone overload—or some wonder drug manufactured in a crack house.

As soon as Megan sped by, he made his move. By the time she realized that she was no longer being chased, Luke had the kid flat on his stomach.

"Luke!"

Megan's horrified cry didn't penetrate the rage that consumed him. He dug his knee into the kid's back and tightened his arm under his chin, pulling the youth's head back. The point of Luke's knife held steady on the boy's frantically beating pulse.

Megan scrambled back and stood over them. "What are you *doing?*"

"Nothing yet," Luke said icily. "I'm about to show a punk what happens when he hurts women on my property."

Waves of fury streamed from him, lapping at Megan, convincing her that Luke was serious. "Luke," she said frantically, "he's my cousin. My *cousin,* for God's sake! Let him go."

Luke turned to face her, his black eyes still savage, so furious he heard only the last few words. "You're too damn softhearted for your own good. You don't have to stay and watch. I'll take care of him."

He looked down at the goggle-eyed boy and gave him a feral smile. "You made a mistake this time, punk. Not only were you running down a woman, you went after mine."

Megan forced herself to speak calmly. "Luke, I'm telling you the truth. This is my cousin Ernie. His sister borrowed my car, so Ernie brought me out here. Please put the knife away and let him up."

Luke stilled, his narrowed eyes focusing on the boy's terrified face.

"Cousin," the kid croaked.

"Cousin?" Luke fractionally eased his grip.

"Cousin," Megan affirmed, sitting down beside the two of them and crossing her legs tailor-fashion. She was still breathless from her sprint, but close enough to grab Luke's arm if she had to.

"Then why the hell were you running?"

She shrugged. "We were just racing. We walked to the back end of the property and decided it would be fun to run back."

"Fun," he said in an expressionless voice.

"Fun." She tapped him on the shoulder with a slim finger. "Now stop being so damned macho and let him up."

Luke swore and pocketed the knife. He rolled off Ernie and lay on the grass, looking up at the sky. "I'm getting too old for this stuff."

"Serves you right," Megan told him in an acerbic voice. "You shouldn't go around sticking knives in people."

"I didn't get a chance," Luke pointed out.

"Don't sound so disappointed."

"Besides, it's just my whittling knife. I couldn't have done too much damage. Just a couple of punctures, if I was lucky."

Ernie paled and jumped to his feet. "Hey, cuz, I gotta go. You sure you want to stay here with this nut?"

Luke gave him a grim look. "Don't push your luck, kid."

"I'll be fine, Ernie." Megan stood gracefully and patted him on the shoulder. She walked a few steps with him, sending him on his way.

Luke waited. The sudden tension in Megan's shoulders was all the warning he needed. All hell was about to break loose, he decided.

She spun around to face him. "Just what are you doing here?"

Still flat on his back, clasping his hands beneath his head, Luke smiled up at her. "I'm the hired muscle you needed."

Eight

"The hell you are!"

Megan stared at Luke, aghast. She had spent two miserable days because of this man—one crying and one futilely wishing she knew something about voodoo so she could stick pins in a very masculine doll—and she wasn't about to start all over.

"We said goodbye two days ago." She glared down at him, infuriated when he simply smiled back.

"*You* said goodbye," Luke said mildly. "I just stood around putting my foot in my mouth."

"What happened to Johnny Penn?" she demanded. "He told me he'd be out here."

"Another cousin?" Luke's brows rose inquiringly. "He's on a paid vacation, compliments of McCall Enterprises."

"You can't do this."

"Who's going to stop me? I'm the boss, remember?"

Luke rolled to his feet, but kept his distance—he didn't want to catch the soft, alluring woman-scent of her. Being around her and keeping his hands to himself was tough enough without asking for more misery. So he'd be careful. Especially since he was already hard, and an erection wasn't exactly the sort of peace offering he'd planned.

At least, not until a few things were settled between them.

Megan scowled and threw him a look guaranteed to freeze Mauna Loa when the lava was running. "It must be nice to have that kind of money."

"It is."

Luke knew if he smiled, he'd be dead on the spot, but he was so glad to see outrage instead of heartbreak in those glorious eyes he could have laughed out loud. Right from the beginning he'd waited for signs of the temper that came with the hair, waited with anticipation, figuring she'd light up like a roman candle when the time came.

Instead, he'd seen her nurturing side, the compassionate, feminine creature with laughter in her eyes—and had been utterly captivated.

Now she faced him like a young Amazon, disdain on her expressive face, her silky mass of hair practically quivering with temper. Luke slid his hands in his back pockets, keeping them away from temptation. Yeah, he decided, she had a temper, and he was going to get it with both barrels.

It was payback time.

"I don't want to work with you," Megan said flatly.

Luke shrugged, keeping his hands where they were. "What you see is what you get."

"You said you'd send me a carpenter."

"I *am* a carpenter."

"A very high-paid one," she said caustically.

Luke shrugged. "I haven't lost my touch." He waited a beat for her anger to flare again before adding, "I can still put in a full day's work."

"I . . . want . . . someone . . . else."

"Tough." Luke felt his temper soaring to match hers and reined it back in. "I'm not sending another man out here to this godforsaken place to be alone with you. What I thought I saw happening a while ago could happen for real, and I'm not going to put you at risk."

Luke swore silently when her eyes flickered at the word. They'd already discussed risk, and he'd failed the test.

Megan eyed him for a long moment, then said quietly, "What's the rest of it?"

He didn't pretend to misunderstand. "I hurt you the other day," he said bluntly. "I didn't mean to, but I did. What I said seemed logical enough to me, but we're obviously not dealing with logic here."

"Brilliant."

He winced. "I'll admit what you've told me sounds like a fairy tale of the first order—" Her lips parted and he held up his hand to stop her. "No, don't get your dander up. I'm trying to say that you're too . . . honorable to lie about it. You've gone for years keeping quiet rather than lying."

"For a very good reason," she said dryly. "People wouldn't believe me."

"Yeah, I know," he said in disgust. "And I'm a prime example of that. The point is, you could have told me a cock-and-bull story about knowing descendants of the original family or that you had a treasure trove of old journals. Instead, you took the risk and told me that you touched walls and heard dead people."

"More or less. For all the good it did me." She gave him a searching look, then turned and began walking toward the front of the house.

Shortening his pace to match hers, he said with dogged persistence, "So, you told me the truth as you believe it, and—"

She stopped and stared at him, openmouthed. "As I *believe* it?" Her hand clenched into a fist and he thought for a second that she was going to slug him. "Thank you very much. Now I'm not a liar, just slightly loony tunes."

"Damn it, will you listen to me?" Exasperated, Luke ran a hand through his hair as she took off again and he followed. "All right, the truth. You told me the plain, unvarnished truth. But will you look at it from where I stand? It's way out of my realm. You might as well have asked me to believe in UFOs."

Megan stopped on a dime and looked up at him, astonished. "Don't you?"

"Don't." Luke watched her tilt her head and seem to study his response. Apparently deciding that it was a warning rather than an abbreviated answer to her question, she asked her own.

"Don't what?"

"Don't change the subject. We're not talking about aliens. Hell, maybe we are—to a degree. I sure felt like I was on alien ground this last week. Honey, I want—"

"Megan," she said coolly. "And no one was forcing you to stay there. You could have gone to your office—"

"—to give you what you want. I—"

"—and made executive decisions all day long. You—"

"—want to believe in what you're doing. But, first—"

"—could whittle to your heart's content without—"

"—I have to understand."

"—being bothered by my loony relatives or—"

"Will you shut up and listen to me."

Her lips still parted to deliver a final withering comment, Megan shut up. Luke hadn't raised his voice, but the sheer intensity of his words got through to her as no shout would have.

Narrowing her eyes to icy blue slits, she said just one word. "What?"

"I'm trying to apologize here." He held up his hand when she drew in a quick breath. "Just hear me out, okay? I don't understand what it is you do when you work. I don't know if I ever will. But I want to try."

"Why?"

"Because it's important to you." *And that makes it important to me.* "I was out of line the other day. I made a judgment call based on my experience, and it hurt you. I'm sorry, I never intended to do that."

Megan studied his face for a long moment. "All right," she said with a small shrug. "I accept your apology. Don't be too hard on yourself—as I said, most people have trouble dealing with this. It probably would have been better if I'd kept on my tap shoes and danced around the subject the way I usually do."

"No." Luke shook his head, his dark eyes determined. "I don't want any lies between us. No evasions."

"Exactly what *do* you want?"

The legend was beginning to look edgy, he thought with relief. The fury was spent and now cold reality was setting in—there was still a job to be done, and he was the only help in sight.

"I want a truce."

Megan stared at him uneasily. "Why? We've settled things already."

"Yeah, and we made a dandy mess of it, didn't we? We have three plantations to restore and two walking wounded to handle them. As far as I'm concerned we're the only two who can do the job right, and we can't do it at all the way things stand now."

Patience, Luke reminded himself, watching the flicker of wariness in her eyes. And keep it strictly business, damn it. Casual would help, too. Yeah, casual was the perfect touch. Anything more and she'd walk away and never look back.

"Well, what do you think?" he prodded, giving her his mildest look. "Are you interested or not?"

"On what terms?"

"Negotiable," he said promptly. "Very. I suggest we keep things simple. You want a week or so to go over the place with a psychic fine-tooth comb so you can get a better feel for the individual rooms." He kept his voice expressionless. "And since you've learned from experience that you frequently need hired muscle to get through walls—I'll be the muscle."

"It seems like an awful waste of your time," Megan commented, her voice carefully noncommittal.

Luke gave an easy shrug. "Actually, it'll help me, too. I want to know as much about the place as you do when we start meeting with the architect."

"We?" She blinked at him, surprised.

"We. I want more than just a report and drawings from you. I want you at every meeting I have with the architect."

He waited while she tried—and failed miserably—to dampen her growing excitement. The legend, he thought again, really was rotten at hiding her feelings.

"That's nice," she said sedately.

His brows went up. "Aren't you usually included in that part of the process?"

"Yes, but I have to fight to get there."

"Not with me."

After a short, strained silence Megan cleared her throat and asked, "Is there anything else?"

Luke nodded. "Yeah, one last thing. I want to know what you learn about each room, as you learn it."

She threw up her hands in exasperation. "Damn it, Luke, you don't believe in anything I do. How can I keep telling you when I know how you feel?"

"You've lived with this all your life, but I haven't been exposed to anything like it before," he reminded her quietly. "And you can't know how I feel, because *I* don't know how I feel. All I can do is promise that I'll keep an open mind. You talk and I'll listen." And keep my opinions to myself. "Now, what are your considerations?"

"*If* we work together, it'll be strictly business." Now her gaze was as direct as a laser. "There will be nothing personal in this relationship. The other night is . . . history. It's over and done with."

But not forgotten, baby. Not by a long shot.

"We treat each other as business associates," she continued steadily. "No more, no less. And at the end of the day we go to our own homes." She lifted her brows and waited for his agreement.

Luke nodded slowly. "How about being friends? Can we manage that?"

"Is that what you really want?"

"Yeah. I do." For starters.

"I don't know." Her gaze was wary again. "Maybe. We'll have to see."

"Okay, we'll see. Anything else?"

"Yes. You don't give the family grapevine any more fodder. As it is, they're going to feast on Ernie's story for a week." She scowled and muttered, "A knife at his jugular, for God's sake."

She focused on his shirt pocket, in deep thought. Finally, apparently satisfied that there weren't any obvious loopholes, she nodded. "Okay. Is there anything we haven't covered?"

Luke shrugged. "Just the usual. Any of the rules can be changed by mutual agreement. Agreed?"

Eyeing him with deep suspicion, Megan slowly nodded.

"Then let's seal the bargain." Luke held out his hand to her.

Megan looked at it as if it were a snake, coiled and ready to pounce. "I trust you," she said finally, turning and heading for the front of the house. She had only gone a few steps when she stopped dead in her tracks.

She turned and looked back over her shoulder at Luke. "Just for your information," she said clearly, "I am *not* your woman."

Whistling softly, Luke followed along behind her. It was going to be a long week.

With luck, it would be just long enough.

"Luke, can you come here for a minute?"

Megan's voice was clear, pitched to be heard over the rain. Every afternoon the clouds raced in, the sky opened up and water poured down, pounding on the roof and saturating the earth. An hour later the sun blazed, creating a steam bath. That was followed by a cooling breeze that swayed the towering palms and delighted the chamber of commerce.

Today, the rain was right on schedule.

"Luke?"

Luke put down the lump of wood that was going to be one of the cottages at the rear of the house and set the knife beside it before he got to his feet. This was the third day he had been responding to Megan's calls, and the way he figured it, if Johnny Penn had been on the job, he would still have been on a paid vacation.

They had explored the attic the first day, testing the beams and flooring. He had been searching for the dry rot and Megan had just touched things. Anything. Everything.

When he'd asked about her fascination with one corner, she had gazed at him in silence.

"They married before the house was done," she'd said abruptly. "They were too much in love to wait. She brought him lunch just after he finished this section of the flooring, and—" Megan looked toward the staircase as if she wanted to be anywhere but where she was "—they made love." She brushed the toe of her sneaker across the several wide boards. "Right here."

The next day they'd crawled under the house, doing much the same thing. The couple had not made love there, she told him when he'd asked, but they'd come damn close to it.

Actually, the rambling old house was in pretty good shape, Luke reflected as he ambled toward the back. He'd checked it over and been fairly certain when he bought it—but he hadn't been sure enough to let Megan visit the place by herself and risk her neck.

It had also been a convenient excuse to stick close to her—that and the whittling project. And he'd been desperate enough to take whatever the gods offered. He still was.

"Luke?"

He grinned at the impatience in her voice. She'd come almost full circle in three days—her original resistance turning to tolerance, then grudging acceptance. This morning she had informed him that as long as she had the highest-paid carpenter on the island at her beck and call, she was going to make him earn his keep.

Yeah, he thought with growing satisfaction, the ends of the circle were getting closer, but it wouldn't be complete until she was back in his arms.

"Luke!"

He followed her voice into the large back bedroom that was going to be part of the new manager's suite and found her standing in a cubbyhole at one side.

"What's up?"

"Where have you been?" Megan turned excited eyes on him. "Look what I've found."

Luke stuck his head in the small, dim room. "A closet?" he ventured. "It's been here all along. Look, honey—"

"Megan," she said absently, running her hands over a shelf just above her head.

"—I know women get excited about storage space, but as closets go, this one's more like a tall doghouse."

"No kidding." Her sideways glance was exasperated. "I know it's bad—so bad, it's an eyesore. And it doesn't fit the rest of the house at all. Our man wouldn't have built something like this."

Luke shrugged. "The next people who lived here probably did it."

"I know they did. It's not part of the original house. I could feel it, even before I noticed the difference in the wood."

"So? It's still ugly." Luke slid his hands in his jeans and teetered back on his heels, wondering how long it would take her to get to the point.

Megan made an impatient sound and turned around to snatch up the floor plan they had made. Unfolding it, she said, "Look. Here's the bedroom next door and here's this one. The closet in the other room is just as skimpy as this one, and the dimensions don't work out."

When he waited, not saying anything, she heaved an impatient sigh. "Come on, Luke. Don't be stubborn. You know what I'm talking about. There's a lot of space left unaccounted for by these miserable little closets."

He eyed the wall, thinking he knew exactly what she was talking about. Trouble. He didn't want to think about it, much less haul in some tools and do something about it. But if the delight in Megan's blue eyes was any indication, they were both going to be up to their shoulders in work.

"You tell me," he drawled.

"We've found a secret room!" she crowed triumphantly.

Luke groaned. "Damn. I knew you were going to say that. I *knew* it." He mentally kissed a quiet afternoon of whittling goodbye.

Megan grinned up at him. "Maybe you're getting psychic."

"Don't even think it," he warned, stepping into the small room and looking around. He put his hands on her shoulders and gently moved her aside. "Actually, I've been waiting for it to happen."

"Waiting?"

"Yeah." Luke ran his hand over the shelf and the wall behind it. "After rubbing shoulders with *kahunas* and someone who reads the past out of chunks of a building, it was the only thing left."

"If you believe that, you have a very limited imagination." Megan stood on tiptoe to peer over his shoulder. "There's nothing in there," she said impatiently, pointing out the obvious. "Why don't you trot outside and fetch your pick and shovel?"

Luke groaned again. "Why?"

"So we can knock a wall down, of course."

"We?" He looked up to check the ceiling. "What do you know about tearing walls down?"

"Enough. I just happen to have several—"

"Don't tell me. Cousins, right?"

"Right. Who just happen to be carpenters. And—" she cast an expert eye over the wall "—I know it's not a bearing wall, so it can come out without the attic falling down on us."

Luke backed out of the confining space, almost stepping on her toes. "Do you know what a dirty job this is going to be?"

"If I said no, I'm sure you'd tell me—every step of the way. But it just so happens that I do know. I've had this done before."

"Plaster dust will fly all over the place," he warned.

"Look at it this way." Her gurgle of laughter was pure mischief. "We aren't expecting company, so we won't have to dust."

Luke propped a shoulder against the wall, a wry grin tucking up the corner of his mouth. "You're really enjoying this, aren't you?"

"Finding a secret room?" Her eyes widened in mock innocence. "Of course."

"And the fact that I'm going to get filthy is just a bonus, right?"

"Well, we both know that I'm the brains of the outfit this week and you're the muscle. Therefore, I get to watch—at a safe distance."

He couldn't help but smile at the look of glee in her eyes. She was loving every minute of being in charge, Luke thought, taking a step toward her just to watch her back away. And he knew he'd be willing to tear down the whole damn house with his bare hands if he could keep her looking like that.

A shaft of alarm crossed her face as he moved closer, and Megan swiped nervously at her shorts, backing up another step. Her working outfit—tank top and walking shorts—was green again today. A nice green, Luke thought appreciatively. Deep. It made her skin look like golden honey. And he knew to his everlasting delight that the rest of her—the covered part—looked just as smooth and soft.

Smooth and soft enough to keep him in a state of half-arousal most of the time.

What the hell was he doing? Before the thought was fully formulated, Luke had eased around and was staring blindly at the wall he was slated to dismantle. There wasn't a thing it could tell him that he didn't already know, but it was the best he could come up with until the blood stopped pooling between his thighs.

Hell. He closed his eyes in disgust. Stalking Megan in the condition he was in was not only stupid, it was a guaranteed invitation to trouble. He—

"Luke?" The laughter was gone from her voice, replaced by doubt. "I was only kidding. I'll be glad to help you with the wall."

"No, you won't." That much he knew for sure.

"Why? I help my—"

"Cousins?" he asked neutrally, looking at her over his shoulder. When she nodded, he forgot patience, forgot pacing, forgot everything he had been telling himself for the last three days. He turned around and let her take a good look at him. All of him.

"Does this look like I consider myself a cousin?"

Megan blinked—at his body's undeniable reaction, as well as the edge of violence in his even voice.

"It's a small room," he reminded her bluntly. "I can't work surrounded by your perfume."

"I don't wear perfume."

"Whatever." He shrugged. "The scent that has your name all over it, the one that reminds me of cool silk and hot sex. And I don't want your breasts and soft bottom rubbing against me every time we move." He stopped, waiting for her to say something. When she didn't, he said, "Aren't you going to ask why?"

Her gaze was still pinned on the zipper of his jeans, and she simply shook her head.

"Because as soon as it happened, we'd be on the floor doing just what we did the other night—only this time we'd be covered in plaster dust. And when we were done, you'd hate me. So I'm not going to take the risk and neither are you."

Megan stepped back, giving him plenty of room when he moved past her and stalked toward the hall. Once he was gone, she released the breath she had been holding. That had been a close call. Very close, if the look in his narrowed eyes was any indication.

And she had no doubt that it was.

The last three days had had more ups and downs than a roller coaster, she reflected, moving a healthy distance from the closet. Part of the furor was because Luke was either transmitting his feelings more strongly or she had become unusually sensitized to him.

Or both.

It had been clear from the start what he wanted. The problem was that she hoped for the same thing. So much that she had agreed to his crazy plan with indecent haste.

Actually, starting from scratch wasn't a bad idea, it just wasn't very realistic, because the slate between them wasn't clear and it never would be. How could she forget the night spent in Luke's arms, being loved until she was exhausted and still wanting more? And his memories were just as vivid, palpable in the very air around them when they were together in the same room.

Even so, his plan had accomplished several things—it had given them both some badly needed breathing space and the opportunity to heal some wounds, as well as strengthening her ability to tune in to Luke. As always, when she considered her psychic ability, she wasn't sure if it was a blessing or a curse.

Things were bad enough without that, she brooded. She already—too much—appreciated his frank masculinity, the male sensuality that tugged at her senses. Add to that the disconcerting erotic flashes she received from him with increasing frequency, and you had a whole bunch of trouble.

She was mulling over the effects of his imagination on hers when Luke returned, carrying a large box of tools and a thick extension cord coiled around his arm.

He set the box down and began emptying it, placing each of the tools on the floor near the closet door. When he finished, he glanced up, looking at Megan inquiringly.

"Something wrong?"

"No," she said too quickly. "Nothing."

Luke had exchanged his jeans and cotton shirt for an older set that had seen hard duty. The jeans were faded and stained, but it was the blue knit shirt that held Megan's undivided attention. It had either been bought a size too small or shrunk in the wash. Whatever the reason, it not only covered Luke, it caressed him, loved him, clung to him, embraced him, emphasizing his powerful shoulders and his taut, hard stomach, delineating every rippling muscle.

If it were a movie, it would be X-rated, she thought, unable to take her eyes off him.

"Megan?" Concern tightened his voice. "What's the matter?"

She shook her head. "Nothing, really. I just..." She broke off with a soft laugh. "That's a great shirt, McCall."

Nine

———

"**E**njoying the show?"

Luke stepped out of the closet with the thick plank shelf and found Megan perched cross-legged on a low table she had dragged in from another room. A cooler of soft drinks sat beside her.

"It's getting off to a slow start," she complained mildly, popping the tab on a chilled can and holding it up in invitation. "But I have hopes."

And the scenery was terrific.

Luke handled the wood plank as if it weighed no more than balsa, but she had watched men tote lumber around most of her life and knew the effort it took. He set it along the floor against a far wall, out of the way, and took the can.

He downed about half of it while Megan watched the muscles of his throat sliding smoothly with each swallow. When her fingers curled into her palms, she knew she was in trouble. She wanted to touch him, to hold the strong col-

umn of his neck between her hands, to catch the trickle of
sweat running down his cheek with a fingertip. And while
she was at it, she just might remove his X-rated shirt as well
as a few flakes of plaster.

Instead, she flattened her hands on her knees and peered
up at him. "Too bad that's not a hunk of wallboard in
there. You could just whang away with a sledgehammer
until it crumpled."

"Did you say you worked with carpenters or a wrecking
crew?"

"They might have been a tad impulsive at times," she
admitted. "But only when they were working on their own
places." When he leaned over to pick up a hammer and
chisel, she groaned. "Luke, it's going to take forever."

He studied her impatient expression and grinned. "It
won't take any longer my way," he promised.

And Luke's way, she knew instinctively, would be to tap
through the finishing coat of plaster to the brown coat—the
precursor of wallboard—which was the fibrous plaster that
stuck to, and filled in the spaces between, the pine laths
nailed to the studs. Once he had a large enough hole, he'd
investigate the space behind the wall and decide where to cut
an opening with his power saw.

He wouldn't use brute strength on the wall any more
than . . . he had on her.

Megan shifted on the low table, wincing at the direction
her thoughts had taken. Although, she admitted silently, she
wasn't surprised. Those kinds of thoughts were never far
away.

Three days of working at Luke's side had seriously un-
dermined her good intentions. It was one thing to say
goodbye to a man believing that any future contacts would
be made over the telephone. It was another entirely to share

an empty house eight hours a day, bumping into him every time she turned around.

She could have managed that part, Megan assured herself, watching what she could see from her vantage point—the muscle in Luke's shoulder bunch and his right arm swing toward the chisel.

No, that wasn't what bothered her. It was the flashes she picked up from him—and the increasing strength with which they were being transmitted. What made it even worse was the fact that he was unaware of them.

His memories of them in bed, naked bodies touching, clinging, entwined, came at the most disconcerting times. His frustration—his need—overwhelmed her at others.

It was darned hard to stay mad at a man who was hurting as much as she was, she brooded, taking another swig of her drink. A man who wanted to repair the damage he had—however innocently—done.

It was especially hard for someone who usually couldn't sustain her anger for more than a few hours.

Sighing, she recalled the conversation she'd had with Devin the night she met Luke, telling him she felt bound to Luke, doubted she could walk away if he needed her.

Well, she had been right. He needed her. He might call it wanting, but she knew need when she felt it.

And, damn it, she wasn't walking.

"Do you think we'll find anything in there?" Megan raised her voice so he could hear over the pounding.

Luke muttered and hit the chisel again. "Sure."

"Really?" Thinking longingly of photo albums and floor plans to show to an unnamed skeptic, she asked, "What?"

"Rat droppings," he said succinctly.

"Luke!"

"I'm not the resident romantic," he reminded her. "I've uncovered too many places like this to have any illusions."

That was the problem, she thought with sudden clarity, aching for the boy whose feelings flowed from the man. He had been a boy who had lost his dreams too early in life. Luke didn't know it, but he wasn't just talking about hidden rooms.

"Luke, what were your parents like?"

After an almost imperceptible beat, the hammer rang on the chisel in a steady rhythm. "Decent people," he said finally, not stopping. "Ambitious. Busy working their way into high middle-class incomes."

Too busy to show their love to a little boy, she knew feeling the loneliness that swept through his memories.

"Then they set their sights on high society."

And they made it. Megan took a ragged breath, wondering if they knew what they had sacrificed to their ambition. And with the image of an imposing stone mansion, surrounded by silence, she had her answer.

They did.

"So, did you do all the preppy things that rich kids do?" She kept her voice deliberately light, knowing precisely how much he disliked her questions. Pretend you're a doctor lancing a boil, she told herself. Let him get some of it out.

"I left home when I was eighteen." His words were punctuated by the blows of the hammer. "I got apprenticed to a carpenter and learned a trade. I told you the rest. Got my contractor's license and had some good luck."

"It was more than luck," she said, raising her voice over the din. "It was hard work. And courage, self-discipline and ambition. Some of which you got from your parents. I imagine they're very proud of you."

"I never went back to ask." Luke grunted and dropped the hammer. Chunks of plaster dropped to the closet floor and dust swirled out behind him. "Would you come here a minute?"

"I thought you'd never ask." Megan jumped to her feet.

"Bring the flashlight with you. And the small step stool."

Megan thrust the light in his outstretched hand and retrieved the stool. "You're too tall to use this," she complained, hitching it closer.

"I know." Luke stepped back out of the way and slid the stool beneath the gaping hole. "That's why you're going to." Before she could do more than blink, he handed her the flashlight, wrapped his large hands around her waist and lifted her up.

He took his time about letting her go, reluctantly dropping his hands only after he was certain she was steady. Megan sucked breath into her starved lungs, wondering if she would always react to his touch with a responding surge of desire, if he would ever be able to conceal his feeling from her.

Putting the troubling thoughts aside, she said, "What do you want me to do?"

He gave her a smile that was all challenge. "You're the psychic in the crowd. Want to try a little test?"

She glanced at the dark hole even with her shoulder, then back at him. "Piece of cake," she said blithely. "Here, I don't need this." She gave him the flashlight, saying, "What do you want to know?"

"Whatever you find out. Wait a minute." He steadied her with a hand on her hip while he pressed closer and thrust his other arm through the hole, reaching overhead, then moving downward until he had completed a large circle. "There." He moved back, letting his hand slide down her thigh. "I just wanted to make sure you didn't run into any spiderwebs."

Megan took a deep breath and made a quick decision, common sense overriding instinct. "Stay close, would you?

I've never done this on a stool, and sometimes the feelings are strong.''

Luke frowned. ''Hell, I never thought about that. Maybe this wasn't such a good idea. Why don't we—''

''Too late.'' Realizing he was about to haul her down, Megan took a quick breath and thrust her arm through the hole.

''Damn it!''

She heard Luke swearing steadily, felt his hands settle on her hips, but then was lost to the sensations sweeping over her.

It seemed only seconds later that he swept her up in his arms and hauled her out of the closet. He swore again, muttering about the dirty floor, and sat her gently on the low table she had used earlier as a chair.

''Stay there,'' he ordered gruffly. ''Don't move a muscle.'' Before she knew it, he was back with a blanket, spreading it on the floor. He picked her up again and settled her on the plaid square, pressing against her shoulders until she was flat on her back looking up into anxious, dark eyes.

''Why did you stop me?'' she asked fretfully. ''I was just getting started.''

''You were there for fifteen long minutes,'' he said through clenched teeth, sitting down beside her. ''You didn't hear a word I said. When you started shivering, I decided you'd been at it long enough. But before I could haul your cute butt out of there, you sagged against me, almost out cold.''

His hand gripped her wrist and he shook it lightly until she opened her eyes. His fingers tightened when he saw how strained they were.

''Listen to me, Megan, and listen well. I never want you to do that again. Do you hear me?''

Wincing, she muttered, "My whole family can probably hear you." She attempted to sit up and was relieved when his big hand held her down.

"Stay right where you are. You aren't going anywhere."

"Luke," she began, "I appreciate your concern, but—"

"*Concern?* You could have broken your arm. You could have fallen and cracked your head."

"That's why I asked you to stay," she muttered, giving him a mutinous glare.

"I'm surprised your family lets you do this alone."

Megan stared at the ceiling in exasperation. "Give me a break, Luke. I'm twenty-six. I don't ask their permission."

"Well, maybe you should," he retorted. "Does Devin know how this affects you?" he demanded.

"He's seen me do this often enough."

"You can't lie worth a damn, so quit trying. How long has it been since Devin's seen you do this?"

Megan shrugged irritably. "I don't write these things on a calendar."

"Take a guess."

"I don't know!"

"A week? A month? A year?"

She heaved an exasperated sigh. "Two or three years."

"And has anything changed since he saw you?"

Megan grimaced. "Are you sure you didn't go to law school?"

"Just...answer...the...damn...question."

"All right! Yes! The reaction is stronger, and I get more tired. Satisfied?"

"Hell, no," he roared, startling her. "I'm not. This is dangerous, and I meant what I said. You can't do it again."

"Luke." She put her hand on his knee in a soothing gesture. "I can't turn this on and off like a light switch. Even if I wanted to stop, I couldn't. It doesn't work that way."

"I don't think I want to hear this," he muttered, calming down as the color returned to her face.

"No, you probably don't," she agreed dryly. "But you're going to, because we're not going through this every time I touch something that's more than a few years old."

She absently brushed some chalky flakes from his knee. "As far back as I can remember, I've had this ability to touch the past, and it looks like I'll always have it. But there's nothing dangerous about it."

Luke's gaze was as skeptical as his words. "That's why you're flat on your back, right? Because there's nothing wrong?"

"The only thing that has changed over the years is that the impressions come faster and clearer, and I get tired—but that's a far cry from being in danger." Megan swallowed dryly and sat up. "I'm fine," she insisted when Luke started to protest.

"What you are is stubborn," he told her, reaching out and snagging the cooler. He took out a chilled can and opened it, handing it to Megan. "Drink," he said quietly.

She blinked and put it to her lips, relishing the cool bite as it slid down her throat. "Thanks."

When her thirst was slaked, she rested the cold can on her knee and gazed at Luke, wincing at his obstinate expression. "I don't know how to say it any clearer. You're just going to have to trust me on this. It's a part of me that isn't going away, but it won't hurt me."

She sighed. He didn't believe her and he wasn't even trying to hide the fact.

"You almost collapsed in my arms a few minutes ago. What would have happened if I hadn't been there?"

"I wouldn't have done it that way. That was your idea, remember?" Megan took another swallow of her drink and tried again. "Look, I'm not stupid. I've seen the difference over the last few years, and I've made adjustments. I always clear a space and sit on the floor. I also seem to have a sensor that tells me when I've had enough."

Luke didn't look reassured. "Terrific. What happened to that famous sensor today?"

"I knew you were there," she said simply. "That you'd take care of me, so I pushed it and stayed a little longer than I should have."

Luke's eyes narrowed. "So you can control it?"

"To a certain extent," she said cautiously.

"And you could possibly avoid it altogether if you wanted to?"

"I don't know. It would be like cutting off one of my arms." She stiffened, her blue eyes clashing with his dark ones. "But that's not the issue here, because I don't intend to find out."

For an instant tension stretched between them, humming and snapping. Luke finally broke the silence. "I won't let you do it again."

Megan stared at him, stunned. "You won't *let* me?" she finally managed. Rage, following on the heels of astonishment, blossomed and erupted. "What the hell do you have to say about it? And how do you think you could stop me?"

"For starters, I could lock this place up tight as a drum and keep you out."

"Don't try it," she warned, her voice shaking with fury. "Because the minute you do, you'll have my resignation. And it won't even slow me down, because there's enough work on this island to keep me busy for the next twenty years."

"Damn it, Megan." Luke surged to his feet and went to stand in the doorway of the closet, staring at the dark hole. Sheer frustration tightened his voice. "Can't you get it through your head that I'm worried about you? I don't know what I'd do if—I don't want anything happening to you."

Megan's eyes softened. "I know." And she did. His feelings were as raw as his words and she was tuned in to every one of them. She got up and went to stand behind him. Touching his shoulder with her fingertips, she could almost feel the adrenaline racing through his body, tightening his muscles.

Closing her eyes, she fought her own battle. She had no right to be mad at Luke for trying to wrap her in cotton and store her away from harm—and life, she reflected moodily. What he wanted to do was no worse than what she had already done to herself. These last five days she had deliberately kept herself insulated from pain—and life. Keeping Luke at a distance had been nothing more than flight. And fright.

But now it was time to make a choice. She could be safe and wonder the rest of her days what she had missed, or she could risk everything on happiness, aware that a lifetime of pain was a definite possibility.

Megan shook her head, knowing there really wasn't a choice. She had never been the type to settle for half a loaf when the whole darn thing was within reach.

Selecting her words with the same care she would have used walking through a minefield, she said, "Luke, I do understand. I'd feel the same way if I thought you were in danger. But you're going to have to trust my judgment on this. I've dealt with it all my life and I know it's safe. I also know my capabilities."

She took a deep breath. "Frankly, letting you back into my life scares me a lot more than any of the psychic stuff I deal with."

It seemed forever before he reacted. For a long moment he didn't even breathe. Then he turned, so slowly she wanted to shriek with frustration. Large hands cupped her face, holding her still while his thumb gently brushed her lips. "Is that where I am? Back in your life?"

Her small laugh was shaky, but her gaze was warm and unwavering. "If we can make it work," she said simply. "If we don't smother each other. If we—"

His lips covered hers in a caress that was as tender as it was thorough. Deepening the kiss, he tugged her closer, holding her so close he could feel her breathless gasp, her breasts, her hips tucked restlessly against his.

"Oh, Megan, I thought—"

"Don't talk." Her voice was a throaty whisper. "Touch me. Show me how—"

His mouth stopped her, turning her words into a sexy purr of pleasure. She nestled closer, sliding her arms around his neck, her hands into his hair, fingers shaping his head, holding him right where he was so he wouldn't stop. Ever.

The pressure of his mouth increased, tilting her head back, parting her lips. His tongue touched hers, went deeper, tasting her, pleasuring her until she shivered.

When she sagged against him, letting him take her weight, he picked her up and headed for the door.

Megan blinked up at him. "Where are we going?"

"To a bed." He stopped, the realization hitting him the same moment her chuckle sent warm breath against his cheek. There were two pieces of furniture in the place and neither of them was a bed.

"Well, hell." He looked at her hopefully. "Want to go to your place?"

"Later," she promised, bringing his head down for another kiss. "I hate to be the voice of reason," she said with a sigh, "but we have a wall to take down."

Luke groaned, but he loosened his hold, letting her slide down his hard body until they were both aching. As soon as her feet touched the floor, Megan moved away, holding him off with an upraised hand.

"No." She shook her head. "You stay right there or we'll never get done. This whole thing started out as a test, remember? I want to tell you about the physical layout I saw before you start on the wall."

"Honey, you don't have to do this. I believe you."

She waved his protest away. "Don't rain on my parade, McCall. I don't get a chance like this very often, and I want to strut my stuff."

Luke subsided, knowing it was more than that. It went far deeper. Megan wanted more than a glib statement of faith from him. She needed his absolute belief and was canny enough to know that hard evidence was the fastest way to get him there.

"The room is about six by eight, just a portion of what it used to be when it was his office. The walls are covered with some kind of grass mat. They started out a pale yellow but have faded to a dull creamy color. The room is empty except for a box or a chest of some kind. I think it's brown, streaked with green and gold. Oh, and there's a little rag doll in the corner by the chest that belonged to one of his daughters. It has a faded red skirt."

She grinned at him, her raised brows returning his earlier challenge. "Now, how about using those muscles and seeing how right I am." She walked over to the wall and drew an imaginary line with her finger a couple of inches above his head. "If you use your power saw along here, you won't hit any nails."

As soon as Luke plugged in the saw, Megan left the room. Nervously, she prowled the house, ending up on the wide front porch, enjoying the fresh breeze and the rain. It had gentled to a sprinkle and the sun was working through the clouds. Just about the time the rain stopped completely, she realized that the house was quiet.

She found Luke standing in the doorway he had just created, shining his flashlight in the small room. He was covered with a fine sprinkling of white dust. The section he'd removed was leaning against the far wall, its grass mat covering a washed-out yellow.

"Come here." Luke held out his hand, taking hers when she reached him. "I think you deserve the honors." He handed her the flashlight and urged her forward.

"It's empty." She spoke softly, as if afraid of disturbing the former residents.

"You knew it would be."

"It's nice to have it confirmed. But, where's—" She played the light around the small room. "Ah, there it is." She knelt beside a small wooden chest, running a questing hand across its elaborately carved surface. "Luke, look." She shone the light on the chest, illuminating what her fingers had already detected—brass trim, gleaming gold where it wasn't green with corrosion.

"Yeah, I see it." He brushed a finger along her cheek. "You're two out of three, so far. One more and you get the jackpot."

Megan switched the beam of light to the opposite corner and held it steady. "Bingo," she whispered.

"I'll take the chest," Luke told her in a neutral voice. "You bring the doll."

They placed their loot on the small table in the full light of the emerging sun, sitting on the floor next to it to gloat.

"Luke, look at this precious porcelain face." Megan delicately stroked the doll's face with her finger. "At least it will be when it's cleaned up. What about the chest?"

"Sealed tight by the corrosion."

Megan groaned, eyeing the deeply carved box with both admiration and dismay. "Damn. How are we going to see what's in it? It's too beautiful to attack with a chisel."

She stopped, studying the warm amusement in Luke's eyes. "What?" she asked suspiciously. She stopped scowling long enough to enjoy Luke's shout of laughter.

"You're the one who just described a hidden room. You can see through walls—why not a box? Just do some of your voodoo stuff if you're so curious."

"There are some things that even I can't do," she said with lofty dignity, then spoiled it by grinning. "Darn it, how do we get it open? I want to see if there are any photos, or something that tells about the family."

"How patient can you be?"

Megan groaned again. "I don't like the sound of this."

"I don't want to force it open," he told her, running a hand over the dusty wood. "Penetrating oil will work through the corrosion, but it'll take a few days. Maybe longer."

"Okay." Megan looked up to find his steady gaze on her, his expression thoughtful, overlaid with a sense of regret. "What?"

"Just thinking," he replied, shrugging.

"Thinking," she repeated, wondering if it would be better to drop the subject. No, she decided. She'd come too far to back down now. "Thinking what? That last week you thought I was weird and now you *know* it? Wondering how fast you can get out of here?"

"No." He reached over and hauled her into his lap, stretching out until he had her pinned beneath him. He dropped a hard kiss on her lips. "Wondering how I could have been so stupid. Wondering how to apologize, and if you can ever forgive me for hurting you."

"Yes." She touched his cheek with gentle fingers. "I can and I do." Her eyes narrowed to blue slits of provocation. "And I would say you're more stubborn than stupid. A real hard nut to crack—but crack you did. Now we start working on the next big item."

Luke eyed her suspiciously but couldn't resist her smiling mouth. He kissed her until they were both breathless, then said, "What item?"

"UFOs."

Ten

———

"Wait, don't put it there! It's too dirty."

Luke nodded and bypassed Megan's dining room table, looking around for a place to put the chest. Megan followed at a leisurely pace, enjoying his wide shoulders, which stretched the blue fabric of his shirt, the line of his back tapering down to lean hips, and the give of muscle in his buttocks. The suggestion of male power was implicit in each step he took. He was hot, sweaty, covered with plaster dust...and she had an overwhelming desire to back him up against the wall and run her hands over him.

All over him.

Age wouldn't change him much, she reflected, glancing at his hair and brows, bleached gray by the dust. It gave her a pretty good idea what he'd look like in twenty years.

Sexy.

Devastating.

"Wait a minute." When they reached the kitchen she hurriedly unfolded some newspapers and spread them on the table, her eyes gleaming with satisfaction when he set the carved box in the centre of them. "I'm glad we brought it here. I want to be around for the grand opening. What kind of oil do we need for the brass?" She looked up and stopped, blinking at the intent expression in his dark eyes. It said explicitly that he wasn't thinking about brass or boxes.

"I, uh, think I only have the cooking kind, but—"

Luke's hand over her mouth stopped her. "I'm staying here with you tonight," he said, making the words a challenge.

Her eyes widened over his fingers. He looked as if he expected her to debate the issue, and was fully prepared to crush any argument she might bring up—even though talking was obviously not high on his list of priorities right now. He'd probably hustled her out of the old house and made it to her place in record time for the same reason. Seduction wasn't the only thing on his mind, she decided. He hadn't wanted to give her time to marshall up any last-minute objections.

It was good thinking, she reflected, but a little late. She had compiled a tidy list of reasons she was better off alone during the two miserable days without him.

Megan kissed his fingers and said, "Yes."

Luke looked at her a long moment, then leaned back on the edge of the table and hauled her closer, groaning with pleasure when she stepped between his spread thighs and clung to him. He lowered his head, fitting his mouth to hers in a deep kiss, trapping her with his arms, keeping her right were she belonged.

When he caught his breath, he said, "Just 'yes'? Want to expand on that a bit—like yes, you were going to lock the doors and keep me in bed for a week?"

"Yes, I want you to stay," she sighed, trailing her fingers up his spine. "And yes, I wonder if we're doing the right thing. Yes, I'm excited, and yes, I'm scared."

"Scared? Why?" He looked at her, appalled. "Of me?"

"No." Her smile was a flash of reassurance. "Never that." She shook her head to emphasize the point. "It's just... damn it, Luke, we hardly know each other, and this isn't exactly a one-night stand we're talking about." She narrowed her eyes. "Or is it?"

"Damn straight it isn't," he said grimly.

"We've known each other less than two weeks, and—"

"Honey," he interrupted, dropping a quick kiss on the tip of her nose, "we'll talk. I promise. Later. All you want. Just let me get a shower first."

But when she tried to step back, his arms tightened pulling her closer.

"Don't change your mind," he ordered fiercely against her temple. "Wait for me."

She heard him take the stairs two at a time and then the bathroom door close. Megan followed slowly, stopping at the guest room, the one Devin occasionally used. She collected some of his clothes and turned to her bedroom, her pace quickening at the sound of water.

Luke was using her bathroom, her shower, deliberately imprinting himself on her territory. His keys were on the bedside table and the covers had been tossed to the bottom of the bed. She raised her brows at the typical—and completely unnecessary—masculine gesture.

Luke had already staked his claim and been welcomed. And she had been imprinted in a far more basic fashion—with his body, holding her, surrounding her, in her.

Self-preservation might occasionally rear its head, produce doubts, but the matter was settled.

She loved him.

She wanted to be with him.

She wanted him tying her to him with bonds that couldn't be broken.

The knob turned easily beneath her hand. Megan stepped inside and took a deep breath, feeling desire swirl along her nerves as she inhaled the steam, the soap, the essence of pure man.

Luke.

Yes, they would talk.

Later.

Much later.

She dropped the clothes on the floor and tugged the end of the ribbon at her nape.

There was no sound audible above the pounding water, no sense of movement, but instinct had Luke turning just as cool air drifted over his body. Megan stepped into the shower, her russet hair sliding over her breasts and falling to her waist.

"I got tired of waiting."

She wasn't complaining. The invitation and desire gleaming in her blue eyes made that very clear. Luke took her hand and brought it to his mouth just as his body reacted with a convulsive shudder. "What took you so long?" he murmured against her fingers.

"I was thinking."

"Bad move." He folded her against him, taking the brunt of the water against his shoulders.

"Then I stopped."

"Good move."

The slow stroking of his hands sent currents of pleasure through Megan, making her shiver and stir restlessly against him. Searing kisses punctuated their breathless words.

"My hair will get wet."

"I'll dry it." Luke's hands settled at her waist, tightened. He lifted her until her breasts were level with his mouth and he touched the tip of his tongue to the hard bead of her nipple.

"Mmm." Megan shuddered at the rush of sensation, a rippling sound of pleasure escaping her parted lips. "Ah, do that again."

He did.

When her hair slid between his mouth and his target, Megan impatiently shoved it aside. "I'm going to cut it all off," she swore, her hands clutching his shoulders, tracing the length of his leg with the arch of her foot.

"Over my dead body."

Luke set her on her feet and looked down into eyes dazed with pleasure. She was incredibly responsive, still discovering her own sensuality, and his own fiercely aroused flesh was testimony to her natural ability.

Fingering a long, fiery tress, he wrapped it around his hand and brought her close for another kiss. "Nice. Very nice. But if we don't get you washed and us out of here," he said, reaching for the shampoo, "we're going to be knee deep in ice water." He overrode her protest upending the plastic bottle. "Watch your eyes."

Washing Megan's hair had to be one of the erotic highlights of a lifetime, he decided, his brisk movements slowing down. She looked like a sprite, with her hands at her nape, beneath the fall of her hair, breasts peaked and body glistening with silver trails of water. He worked his fingers through the soapy froth, piling her hair in a precarious mound atop her head. When it tumbled down, leaving dabs of foam in its wake, he used his hands as a washcloth, stroking, kneading, palming the soap over her entire body.

They were both breathing hard by the time he stepped aside and thrust her under the spray, carefully rinsing the soap out of her hair.

"Come on, let's get out of here."

He opened the door and bundled her out, tossing her a towel for her hair. While he rubbed himself briskly with another, he watched, mesmerized, as Megan bent at the waist, sending her hair tumbling over her head to the floor and his pulse rate scrambling. It also made her breasts bounce and her bottom tighten in a way that cut off his breath. She used the towel as a turban, twisting it and letting it trail down her back when she straightened.

Luke tossed his towel aside and reached for a dry one, holding it open for Megan. When she reached for it, he shook his head, saying softly, "My pleasure."

Megan's initial confusion was lost in a haze of pleasure. She moved sinuously when the terry cloth skimmed down her back, shivered when it brushed her hardened nipples. And when it pressed the mound beneath the gentle curve of her belly, her voice cracked in an involuntary whisper.

"Oh . . . Luke."

He hunkered down and dried first one leg, then the other, the touch of his large hands exquisitely tender. When he was finished he dropped the towel on the floor and placed his hands on her hips and, urging her closer, dropped a soft kiss on her belly.

Before she could say a word, he surged to his feet. Swinging her up in his arms, he took her into the other room and dropped her gently in the center of the large bed, following her down.

The turban fell off just before she landed, and her damp hair belled out, spreading like a fiery fan on the pale sheet.

Luke propped himself on his elbow and gathered a handful of shiny strands, letting them slide through his fingers.

"I imagined you like this the first time I saw you."

Megan blinked up at him. "Naked?"

"Mm-hmm. With you hair wild and wrapped around both of us."

"Were you naked, too?"

He grinned. "What do you think?"

"Probably."

"Definitely."

Megan frowned thoughtfully. "Do you mean that first day you came out? When I opened the door?"

"Before that. When I was standing out in front, waiting for you to get rid of your cousins."

"Luke, you didn't even know me!"

"Shocking, huh?" he said complacently, rubbing several silky strands between his fingers.

"Scandalous."

"That, too."

Megan turned her face into his hand, rubbing her cheek against his palm like a kitten asking to be petted. "You know what?"

"Hmm?"

"You have some very interesting fantasies, McCall."

"They got better with time."

She reached up and touched his lower lip with the tip of her finger, smiling when he gently nipped it. "I love bedtime stories," she said huskily. "Want to tell me one?"

Luke looked down at her smiling eyes and tempting mouth and felt his heart swell. "I've already done better than that."

Her eyes widened. "When?"

"The last time we were in this bed. I *showed* you."

After a beat, Megan's eyes rounded in innocent amazement. "Really? Are you sure?"

He nodded, waiting.

"Luke," she said hesitantly, "there's something I think you need to know. It may not be really important, but then again, maybe it is. I haven't said anything, because—"

"Hell!" Luke stiffened and glared down at her. "What? What little thing haven't you told me? That you really *do* see UFOs? That you went on a spaceship? You had a luau for some little green men? Come on, Megan—I figure by now I can handle just about anything."

"Maybe you won't think it's important, but—"

"For God's sake, *tell* me!"

"It's my memory," she said, giving his arm a soothing pat.

"Memory?" he repeated blankly.

"Memory. I have this glitch—just a little one—that makes me forget things."

"What the hell are you talking about? You have a memory like a computer."

"That's the sad part," she said mournfully. "It's very selective. Usually it happens when someone shows me something. They have to do it over and ov—"

Luke groaned and rolled on his back, slipping an arm beneath Megan and hauling her along with him. "Damn it, woman, don't ever do that to me again."

"Scared you, huh?" She arranged herself comfortably, sprawled along his length. "Well, for your information, I haven't seen any little green men." She waited for him to relax before she added, "Yet. But if you ever change your mind, I know a perfect place to go at dusk. It's high and you can see for miles."

He shook his head. "This is the only place I want to be. Right here, looking at you." He lifted her higher, so her

mouth was level with his, and tangled his hand in her hair.
Bringing her head nearer to his, he touched her lips with the
tip of his tongue, testing the softness, the waiting, the invitation.

"Yes?" he asked against her mouth.

She nodded, growing still when his teeth closed with exquisite care on her lower lip. When a shiver rippled through
her body, she felt him smile.

"You like that?" she whispered.

"I like making you shiver, feeling you melt like honey all
over me." He raised her higher, touching her tight, sensitive bud with his tongue, his own body hardening at her
broken cry. His mouth closed on her breast, drawing on the
pink nipple, holding it in the gentle vise of his teeth, stroking it with his tongue. Turning his head, he captured her
other breast, savoring the textures, the tight beaded center
of sensation.

Megan whispered his name with every breath she took,
arching her back to get closer to the source of magic that
was sending shafts of tension curling through her body. Her
hands were braced on the mattress above his shoulders, her
legs shifting restlessly. "I want—"

"What?" He lifted her so he could see her flushed face,
watch her breasts rise and fall with her quick breathing.
"What do you want?"

"You. All of you." She moved again, restlessly, freezing
when her thigh brushed against his aroused flesh. Luke
groaned and settled his hands at her narrow waist, then
worked down her hips and thighs to her knees, drawing
them higher, until she straddled his hips.

When she sat up, he smiled, his eyes gleaming with anticipation. "Then take me. As much as you want, however you
want."

He thought again of a young Amazon. She sat astride him, her elegant spine straight as a poker, her breasts firm. Her cinnamon hair tumbled forward over her shoulders, parted at her breasts to reveal honey-colored flesh and hard pink nipples, and flowed down to slide over his chest.

Megan blinked, a smile of sheer speculation curving her lips. Luke's lean body was like a stallion's between her thighs, all sizzling heat and controlled energy. She leaned forward, resting her palms on his chest, her fingers furrowed in the mat of crisp dark hair.

"Whatever you want," he reminded her, catching his breath when her fingers found a flat nipple. He twisted beneath her hands, increasing the pressure of her touch. "Yeah, honey, that's it. Just like that."

Megan's nails sank into him lightly as she kneaded his warm skin and hard muscles. Her hands roamed down to his flat stomach and up again, enjoying his warm body and the approval gleaming in his dark eyes. It warmed her as his hands stroked her, moving slowly from her knees to her breasts.

Megan drew in a sharp breath and held it, unable to move when his thumbs grazed her nipples. The sensation of being surrounded by Luke was having a dizzying effect on her. He was burning beneath her, between her thighs, one hand caressing her breast and the other on her back, urging her down for a hot, deep kiss.

She shuddered and his arms briefly tightened around her, then he helped her sit up, supporting her. When she was steady, his hands worked down to her waist, her belly. Then lower.

She shivered, reaching back to touch his thighs, stilling as unutterable tension filled her. "Luke?"

"I'm right here."

"Mmm."

"Yeah."

"Oh!"

"Again?"

"Yes . . . yes . . . *yesss!*"

Megan's broken cry told Luke all he needed to know. She was as ready as he was, wanted him as much as he wanted her, needed him as no one ever had.

Him.

No one else.

Exultation filled him at the thought. The Amazon—the legend—wanted him.

He rolled over, taking her with him. Leaning over her, he controlled her feverish movements with his body, while he reached for the bedside table, finding a small packet next to his keys. When he turned back, Megan slid her arms around his neck.

"Now," she whispered, wrapping her long legs around him, holding him closer. "Now."

"Now," Luke agreed. Holding her gaze with his own, he slid into her softness muffling her soft welcoming cry with his mouth.

Megan shivered, tightening around him, pleasure rippling through her in rhythmic waves. Arching to be closer, closer. Clinging, their bodies slick with sweat. The waves grew bigger, stronger, pleasure almost pain, and her body convulsed, drawing him deeper, holding him. And then Luke swallowed her cry and gave in to his own shattering release.

Later, Megan lay with her head tucked on his shoulder, her arm across his stomach, an occasional aftershock shivering through her.

"Luke?" She smiled when his arm tightened around her waist.

"Hmm?"

"Are you awake?"

"I am now."

"I just wanted to tell you..." Her voice faded as she stretched, moving languidly against him.

Luke waited. "Tell me what?" he prompted finally.

"That..." Megan yawned. "That was wonderful."

"Mmm."

"You were wonderful."

"Hell on wheels," Luke agreed complacently. He opened his eyes and gazed up at the lazily looping overhead fan, touched to the depth of his soul. Touched by the trusting way she gave herself to him, by her generosity, and—possibly most of all—by her belief in him.

"Luke?"

"Mmm?"

"Now you're supposed to tell me that I was wonderful."

Tendrils of panic snaked through Luke. He had never said that to a woman in his life. He had never felt it in his life—until Megan. It wasn't that he was simply out of practice, it was that, he had never learned. Some men could write poetry to a woman like Megan, others could compose a song. She deserved a man who would rhapsodize over her, not one who didn't have the first idea how to say the things she wanted to hear.

But she didn't have another man, he told himself grimly. She had him and, by God, she wasn't going to get the chance to go looking for someone else.

Before the panic could grow, Luke turned on his side, holding her captive in the circle of his arm. Dropping a kiss on the tip of her nose, he said lightly, "You were... magnificent. Sexy. Glorious. Sexy." Teasing kisses punctuated the words. "Tempting. Sexy." His lips lingered longer, trailing down her throat to her breast and back again. "And utterly enchanting."

Megan blinked up at him. "Gosh, *wonderful* would have been just fine." She touched her fingers to his cheek, gently, tenderly, then nestled against him. "Now you can go to sleep."

They closed their eyes, and both of them knew he meant every word he had said.

Eleven

___

"Devin, I'm fine. Really." Megan's fingers tightened on the receiver. "Quit being such a fussbudget."

"You'd be one, too, if you were in my shoes," he drawled through the telephone line. "You've been like a damned roller coaster these last few days, and I'm getting a little queasy from all the ups and downs. On top of that, you haven't been returning my calls."

"I'm a working girl, remember? I've been out at the plantation every day, working my drawing fingers down to the bones."

"Alone?" His voice sharpened. "I don't like the idea of you being there by yourself."

"Then you can rest easy. I've got a bodyguard, who is also a carpenter and a very handy handyman. On loan from McCall's."

"Luke." His voice fell somewhere between neutral and hostile.

"Luke," she agreed, looking through the open doorway to the kitchen where Luke sat at the table, brushing oil on the brass trim of the chest.

Devin sighed. "Damn. No wonder you've been so... Look, I don't know how to say this, but—"

"Then don't," Megan said gently. "Just pull the shades, little brother." She waited, wondering how he would react to the phrase they'd coined years earlier when they'd discovered a need for some privacy, even from each other. It was, they had found, politer than a blunt *butt out*. Over the years, Megan had frequently found herself on the receiving end of such advice, but it was Devin's first experience.

"Meg . . . Oh, hell."

"I'm all right," she assured him. "And if things turn out . . . not all right, I'll still be all right."

After a long moment, he said, "I had to untangle that. I know you will. Just remember, Sunshine, I'm always here if you need me."

"I know. I always have known and I always will."

Megan cradled the phone just as Luke came through the door, wiping his hands on an old cloth.

"Who was that?"

"Devin."

His brows rose. "Is your watchdog checking up on you? Or me?"

She took the question seriously because she couldn't tell what was going on behind his thoughtful expression. "Both. Do you mind?"

"Nope." He dropped a swift kiss on her lips, keeping both the oily cloth and his hands away from her blue shirt. "It's a protection you're lucky to have."

"And you?"

He grinned. "Your brother and I understand each other."

Eyeing him suspiciously, she said slowly, "Exactly what does that mean?"

"It means that he laid out the ground rules the night we met." Luke gave his hands a last swipe and stuffed the cloth in the back pocket of his jeans. "Want to go for a swim? It's warm, and there's a full moon," he said temptingly.

Megan didn't have to think about it. "Sounds good. What do you mean, ground rules?" She allowed him to take her elbow and hustle her up the stairs.

"I suppose you'll want to wear a suit."

"Of course I will."

"I don't get it." He kicked off his shoes and watched her pull her bikini off a closet hook. "You sleep with me, you shower with me, you get undressed in front of me, but you won't swim without a suit."

"That's because I'm weird," she said calmly, pulling her shirt over her head. "Luke—"

"Yet you told me you swim in the nude when you're alone."

"I do."

"Then why—"

"Because when you're here, I'm not alone," she said with unassailable logic. "Luke—" She stopped, her breath catching as it always did when he undressed.

He peeled down his jeans, taking his briefs along with them, and kicked them off. The shirt went next, leaving him unabashedly and magnificently male. Dustings of dark hair covered the hard muscles and warm, resilient skin that felt so good beneath her hands.

Luke pulled on a sleek, navy blue suit and looked up. "Ready?" His expectant expression changed to a grin. "You're staring, blue eyes."

"Ready."

He gestured toward the door, amused both by her flushed cheeks and testy reply. The legend was a constant delight. He never knew from one minute to the next if he'd be dealing with the Amazon or her counterpart.

Megan led the way to the pool, aware that Luke deliberately lagged behind, wondering if she would ever grow accustomed to the way his gaze touched her body with an almost physical impact. And how her body jumped in response.

Probably not.

She hoped not.

She also knew he was deliberately trying to distract her. He didn't want to answer a very simple question.

When they stood at the deep end of the pool, she said, "All right, Luke, quit tap-dancing. What ground rules?"

"Actually, it was only one." He grinned, apparently in fond remembrance of the incident.

"Well?" She tapped her bare foot on the decking.

"He said if I didn't keep you happy, he'd kill me." He waited for fury to darken her eyes. He wasn't disappointed.

"*Kill* you?" She was speechless for all of three seconds. "And you think it's funny? You're as crazy as he is! Do you have any idea how dangerous my brother is under that smile of his? He's trained in about every kind of martial art that exists, and—"

Luke held up a pacifying hand. "He wouldn't do it," he soothed.

"Of all the stupid, macho, terminally male attitudes I've seen in a lifetime of living with Murphy men, this takes the cake. He's nuts and you're no better!" She stopped glaring for a moment and drew in a deep breath. "How do you know he wouldn't?"

"Because I wouldn't let him," he said mildly.

The glare returned. "Wonderful. And I suppose you think you—"

"Could stop him."

The skepticism in her eyes slowly faded as she took another look at him. Luke stood there with a faint smile on his face, and she remembered Ernie with a knife at his throat. Even though Ernie wasn't exactly world-class competition, she suddenly had no doubt that he could do exactly what he said he could.

A blend of fright and fury poured through her at the thought of the two of them in combat—and she knew with chilling certainty that if it ever reached that point, it would be a real battle. The thought of either Luke or her brother being hurt was simply too painful to bear.

Anger was easier to deal with, so she allowed it to return full force. Thus fortified, she did exactly what she would have done if Devin had been standing next to her, smiling the same annoying smile that Luke was aiming at her. Putting her whole body into it, she shoved—and watched Luke topple like a tree into the water.

He made a very satisfactory splash.

It would have been even more gratifying if he had floundered for a while, but Luke swam with the silence and efficiency of a shark. He came up without a ripple and raked his hair back. "Feel better?"

She bent over, hands on her knees, watching him. As usual, she couldn't tell what he was thinking. "A little."

Without warning, Luke's hand closed around her ankle and tugged. She landed next to him with a splash that sent water surging over the side of the pool.

She came up beside him, spluttering.

He smiled. "Me, too."

Luke reached out and dragged her up against him, holding her so tight she let out a squeak of protest. Kissing the silver drops of water from her face, he said in a voice so tender it brought tears to her eyes, "I'd never hurt your brother, sweetheart. Any more than I'd hurt you. I know how important he is to you."

Trusting Luke to keep them afloat, she slid her arms around his neck, flinching as she tapped into feelings that were as chilling as cold fingers on her spine. Alone, they said. Always alone. Accepting it, expecting nothing more.

"And you?" she murmured, nuzzling his cheek, her lips close to his ear. "Could you keep from getting hurt? I wouldn't handle it any better if anything happened to you."

Shock and sheer, absolute disbelief jolted through him into Megan. No one had ever worried about him. At least, not as far back as he could remember.

For an instant Megan was consumed by rage at the thought of parents who had ignored a boy, depriving him of a vital part of life. It was no wonder Luke had perfected his poker face, she reflected as she recovered. The man was a walking, talking mass of emotions kept tightly leashed. Of course, without the ability to shield himself, he never would have made it in the business world as he had. Big-time.

But the downside of his control was loneliness. He never trusted anyone, not even—

Her thoughts were sent flying when Luke lifted her as if she weighed no more than a flower and sat her on the edge of the pool. With an effortless surge, he was out of the water and on his feet. He grabbed her hand and pulled her up beside him.

Swinging her around to face him, he said curtly, "You don't have to worry about me. I can take care of myself."

Megan didn't know which was worse—tuning in to the emotions that tore at her heart or dealing with an arrogant, idiotic man. "Yeah. Sure you can. Well, I will worry. I make a habit of worrying. I *like* to worry. I just don't want to see you hurt, okay?"

"Why not?"

For once, his poker face wasn't working, Megan noted absently. Hope struggled with searing doubt and anxiety, and the battle was reflected in his eyes.

One of them was going to have to take the first step, Megan brooded. One of them was going to have to say flat out what was crying to be said. One of them had to take the risk.

And guess who it's going to be, she thought morosely. The one who has a family support system the size of New Hampshire, that's who. The one who knows what's at risk, but can't live with the alternative, that's who.

Oh, hell.

She touched his mouth with her fingertips, gently. "Luke, I don't know any woman who wants the man she loves mangled or mutilated."

Shock paralyzed him. "Loves?" he finally managed.

"Loves." She tilted her head, studying his face, and almost wept. Then anger—swift and glorious—swept away her incipient tears. "What on earth did you think was going on here? You brought your clothes over, you have a key to the house and you sleep in my bed—at my invitation. I'm twenty-six years old, for heaven's sake, and those are three firsts in my life." She stalked past him, working herself into a fine fury. "Or did you think I had a revolving door? That I invited any man who looked at me twice to—"

Luke caught up with her and pulled her back against him, holding her around the waist while his teeth closed with exquisite care on the soft flesh of her nape. "No, spitfire, I didn't think that. I know how lucky I am."

Megan closed her eyes, savoring the feeling of her body pressed against his, feeling his heat and arousal.

"What I don't know is why you didn't say anything about love before this."

The logical question merely fanned the flame of her fury. Pushing his hand away, she said, "Why? *Why?* Well, I had a few fairly good reasons." She turned in the circle of his arms and glared at him, jabbing a finger in the air. "One, I didn't know how you felt." Another finger joined the first. "Two, I was being noble, because I didn't want to embarrass you. Three, once I figured out what was going on, I didn't want to scare you off. And four, I had the crazy idea that you should say something first."

Temper still riding high, she said, "You decide, McCall. Take your pick."

Savage exultance ran through him, along with the knowledge that she was well and truly ticked. But she wanted him. She *loved* him. Luke swung her into his arms, holding her high against his chest. "I take them all," he said softly. "Every last one of them. And you. Most of all, I take you." Megan looked up at him, her smile almost bringing him to his knees.

She gave his shoulder a quick kiss of approval as he carried her over to a wide lounge chair. Waiting until he lowered himself in a casual sprawl, keeping her in his arms, she asked, "How do you take me?"

"What?" Luke raised his lips from the curve of her breast and looked up, groaning silently. Her incredible eyes were wide with expectancy, and she looked as if she had settled in for one of those discussions that women seemed to love— the intimate kind.

"I said," she repeated patiently, "how do you take me?"

"Any way I can get you," he said promptly, and knew by the withdrawal in her eyes that it was the wrong answer. Megan stayed in the circle of his arms, but a thoughtful expression had replaced the wild joy.

"Luke, I'm serious about this. I love you. I wouldn't have made love with you if I didn't, but I haven't the foggiest idea how you feel about me."

"What the hell do you mean?" His hands tightened on her shoulders as if she was already trying to slip away. "I let you know from the beginning that I wanted you. The first damn day we met."

"You're right." She nodded slowly. "I've always known you wanted me."

Luke relaxed. "So that's settled."

"No." She shook her head. "It's not. I think we need to define some terms here. For instance, I—"

"Sweetheart—"

She held up her hand to stop him. "No, just listen a minute. This is important. To both of us. I know what I mean when I say I love you. I mean I want to share my life with you. I want to marry you and have your children. I want to grow old together, maybe restore more homes together and watch our grandchildren grow like flowers on a vine."

Luke caught her hand and brought it to his lips, unutterably touched. "Megan—"

"Wait. There's more. I haven't the foggiest idea what you mean when you say you want me. For how long? Until someone with a cuter tush walks by? How deep do your feelings go, Luke? Did you take one look at me and think I'd be okay for a one-night stand? And later, was it good enough to be considered an affair? Are we having an affair? If so, how long does it last?"

"What the hell are you talking about?" Luke rolled to his side, dumping her on the cushion next to him. He planted a hand near her shoulder and scowled furiously down at her. "When have I ever given you the impression that you're a cheap little tart, there for the taking? When? Just... tell...me...when."

"Never." Megan turned her head and kissed his wrist. "When I'm with you I feel protected, and cherished. I trust you with my life. I know that you want me, desire me. And I feel . . . loved." Megan took a shaky breath. Even for her, beneficiary of so much love, this wasn't easy.

"You feel loved?" Luke asked, treading his way through unfamiliar territory. He swore silently, wishing he knew how to remove the doubt in her eyes.

She nodded, reaching up to touch his cheek. "At times, very."

The words soothed Luke as much as the touch of her soft fingertips. Relief poured through him, easing the knot in his stomach. "Good. That's exactly the way I want you to feel. Cherished, protected and loved. Now, are we on track?"

Megan heaved a gusty sigh. Deprived or not, the man was *thick*. "No, we're not. Listen to me. I said I feel loved. That's true. But I don't *know* that I'm loved, and that makes all the difference in the world. And," she continued, enunciating clearly, "I hate to beat a dead horse, but I don't know it because you haven't *said* it." Unable to conceal her exasperation, she said, "Are we speaking the same language here?"

The knot moved up to his chest, cutting off the air in his lungs. Luke knew he was in danger of losing the best thing he'd ever had. Megan was shredding her pride, holding her heart in her hands, asking for a few simple words. Words that would change her life. Hell, who was he kidding? Change *his* life.

Their lives.

"No. I don't think we are," he said finally, his voice strained, wondering if stark honesty would be enough for her. "I don't know how to talk about emotions. I never heard the language and I sure as hell never learned it. For all I know about it, it could be Chinese." He dropped his head and brushed his lips over hers. "But, sweetheart, you can take this to the bank. When I say I want you, I mean it with everything in me."

Megan almost melted. She almost told him that was good enough and let it go at that.

Almost.

But if she did, she would be cheating both of them. She would spend the rest of her life trying to interpret his actions, and he would be deprived of the dubious pleasure of baring his soul and waiting to see if it would be shredded by a careless word. Redeemed when it wasn't. Most of all, he would be deprived of removing all her doubts and making her a very happy woman.

"That's good to hear," she said softly, touching his hand. "Very good." Steadying her breath, she shook her head and added, "But not good enough. Luke, I'm a romantic. I know I am. But I'm not fool enough to spend however much time we have together convincing myself that you love me simply because I *want* you to love me."

"However much time we have together," he repeated slowly, his gaze enigmatic. "Planning on ending it already?"

"Give me a break here," Megan snapped, pushing him away and sitting up. Scooting down to the other end of the cushion, she crossed her legs lotus fashion and scowled at him. "I'm trying to make a point. For instance, how do you see this thing—relationship, for lack of a better word—we have going for us? Is it temporary? To be ended whenever one of us throws in the towel? Or is—"

"It's permanent," he snarled, looking as if he wanted to throttle her. "No other man for you, no other woman for me."

"Thank you."

Her smile almost knocked him sideways, and he groaned, realizing how anxious she'd really been.

Megan figured she was on a roll, but damn, it was hard work. "So how do you see this permanent thing we have here? A modern arrangement of two single adults cohabiting? Or something more exotic like—"

"Marriage."

It was a single word, more of a command than a request, but it was the music of celestial harps as far as Megan was concerned. However, elated as she was, she decided he still had a way to go before he won the trophy. An easy win was no win at all as far as Lucas McCall was concerned.

"You think marriage is exotic?" she asked, widening her eyes.

Luke's patience was gone—and he couldn't wait another minute to have her back in his arms. He reached for her hand and tugged, groaning in relief when she flung herself at him, tumbling them back on the wide cushion. "If it's ours," he said confidently, "it's bound to be. And erotic."

He kissed her, holding her in place with the weight of his body, smiling against her mouth when her hands slipped around his neck. When their breathing steadied, he said, "So when are we going to get married?"

Megan opened love-drenched eyes and met his dark, waiting gaze. "Anytime you want," she said in a tranquil voice. "After you tell me you love me and *ask* me to marry you."

He stared down at her for an endless moment. "Does that mean we're not sleeping together anymore?"

Megan's arms tightened around his neck, hearing the caution in his voice. He sounded as if he expected a scene of high drama, ending with an order to pack his bags and leave. "Did you hear me say anything that crazy?" she demanded, shrieking when he swooped her off the lounge and swung her around.

"Come on, Amazon. Let's go to bed."

The next morning, wearing jeans and a towel around his neck, Luke grinned at his reflection in the mirror, contemplating life while he ran an electric razor over his dark beard.

It was good. Damn good.

Megan was still sleeping with him. In fact, she had spent the night sleeping *on* him, her hair sliding over him, binding them together.

Together.

She wasn't kicking him out and she wasn't worried. As far as she was concerned, everything was settled. When he wanted a wife, all he had to do was tell her he loved her and propose.

Sounded simple enough, he thought, his smile fading. But then, so did cliff diving and bungee jumping. He knew it could be done—he just couldn't see himself doing it.

He was drying his face when Megan poked her head in the room. "Luke, do you know an Alan Jamison?"

He groaned. "He's an old friend and the manager of my San Francisco hotel. Tell him I'm not here." He checked her out in the mirror and decided she looked fine. A bit drowsy and her silky hair tousled, but that just added to her sleepy-kitten look. Best of all, she looked content. She looked like a woman who had spent the night exactly where she wanted to be—in the arms of her man.

Her man.

He blinked thoughtfully at the possessive implication, then shrugged. He had never been the possessive type, but Megan had changed all that.

She was his.

And, by God, he was hers. She had chosen and claimed him, and she was stuck with him.

"Too late. I already spilled the beans." Megan gave him a long, black look. "And just how did he get this number?" she demanded. "Did you take out an ad in the paper announcing that you're now sleeping at the Murphy place?"

"Not yet. I thought I'd do that this afternoon." When she menaced him with narrowed eyes, he reached out and pulled her into his arms, letting his hands drift down to her hips, savoring the soft glide of fabric that ended at her thighs. "Just kidding. I left this number at the hotel for emergencies. No name—just a number." His hands followed the material back to two thin straps over her shoulders. "What is this thing?" he asked, dark eyes gleaming.

"A nightshirt," she said breathlessly. "And speaking of emergencies, Mr. Jamison seems to think he has one."

"Tough. Remind him I'm on vacation."

"I tried, but I have a feeling he doesn't believe you do things like vacations. And I think the funny noise I heard was him biting off his fingernails."

"Well, hell," Luke sighed, tossing the towel on the countertop.

When he returned, Megan had just stepped out of the shower and was reaching for a towel. She looked up and her hand stilled. "You have to leave."

Luke winced at her expressionless voice. It wasn't a question, and she didn't seem to care one way or the other. Then he saw the bleak expression in her eyes and he started to breathe again. He could deal with misery and pain, any damn thing except indifference.

"He has union problems that could tie up operations for several months. I have to go back for a while," he told her, watching her methodically dry the moisture from her body. "Megan, honey—"

She shook her head and curved her lips in what was meant for a smile. It was a miserable failure. "Don't worry about us while you're gone," she told him. "We'll talk when you come back."

If *you come back.* The unspoken words rang in the silence between them.

She dropped the towel and walked into his arms, fragrant with the scent of the water, ginger and woman. "You'll take care of yourself?"

"I'll be back, damn it." His hands tightened around her waist, holding her against him.

Megan covered his chest with tiny kisses. "When do you leave?"

"Four hours. Come with me."

She shook her head. "I'll be better here, working."

"A week at the most. That's all I'll be gone," he promised, lifting her chin so she could see the truth in his eyes. "Five days if I'm lucky. Four with a miracle."

"Do you have to pack?"

"Pack?"

"You know—clothes." She lifted her shoulders in a small shrug. "Stuff."

"No. I always keep things at the hotel."

Megan's sigh was filled with relief. "Then we haven't quite run out of time."

She took his hand and led him back to the bedroom.

Twelve

We haven't run out of time.

Yet.

Luke heard the echoes of Megan's words on the flight to San Francisco and during the interminable meetings he attended when he landed. Each time, they were followed by her unspoken qualification.

Yet.

After three days of listening to arguments, he began cutting red tape with ruthless efficiency, forcing concessions by both sides, racking up an equal number of debts and favors over the next two days.

The morning of the sixth day, with barely time to make an early meeting, he white-knuckled the telephone receiver as he listened to the distant ringing. She hadn't been there the last three times he'd called.

With the time difference, Megan should still be in bed, curled on her side, hair spilling like a banner across the pillows—and answering the damned phone. She had an extension on the bedside table and usually managed to catch it on the second ring. He had once teased her about being the quickest draw in the West, and her pensive reply had sobered him—with a family as large as hers, she'd said, there was always a chance that someone needed help.

If she was there, she always answered the phone.

When the answering machine kicked in, he said, "Where the hell are you? It's too early to be anyplace but in bed. And even if you're working, you should be in your office. Megan, so help me God, if you're doing something crazy, as soon as I get back, I'll lock you in that gorgeous house of yours and throw away the keys. You have my number—call me. If I'm not here, leave a message."

His dark brows drew together in a frown as he thought of all the possibilities—she didn't want to talk to him, she'd slipped in the shower and broken her leg, had been run over by a bus, had fallen in one of the steaming craters that dotted the island.

"I'll be back in a couple of days at the latest," he promised, wincing as he remembered saying that a few days earlier. "We'll have that talk. Everything will work out fine. And, sweetheart, I . . . miss you."

Wondering what she was doing, and looking forward to bawling her out in person, he took the elevator to the main floor to meet Alan Jamison. For the next three hours, while they discussed their options and plotted a course of action, Luke ignored a nagging feeling of uneasiness, telling himself that Megan was a rational adult.

Most of the time.

She wouldn't do anything foolish.

Of course, the difference between her definition of foolish and his left a lot to be desired.

She kept her wits about her.

Unless she was wandering around in the past.

Damn it, he should have made it crystal clear that she wasn't to visit the plantation without him. He had told her three times and she had given him her patented patient look, but . . .

Maybe she hadn't been listening.

Maybe she had nodded, knowing damn well she was going to head out there as soon as he took off. He wouldn't put it past her.

And maybe she had fallen into a deep, dark hole and couldn't get out.

In the middle of his lunch, Luke surged to his feet and dropped his napkin on the table. "Alan," he said abruptly, "I'm going back to Hawaii. This is your baby now. You know as much as I do, so just do the best you can."

The slim, brown-haired man looked at him, his brows shooting up in surprise. A gleam of anticipation filled his hazel eyes. "What if I botch it up?"

"Then I'll make sure you deal with the mess for the next twenty-four months—the remainder of your contract."

Jamison gave a crack of laughter. "Can I reach you at the same number?"

"No." The answer surprised Luke as much as it did his friend. "I don't want to be bothered."

"For how long?"

"I'll let you know. If the place burns down, call the insurance company, not me."

Luke went to his room and made two telephone calls. After the first, he hung up and swore. Devin was in Seattle. The second was to a charter airline.

An hour later Luke was on a flight to the island, wondering how long it would take a woman like Megan to decide she didn't need a man in her life. Especially a man who couldn't manage to say three simple words.

A lot less than six days, he decided grimly.

What was a woman to do when her two favorite men were out of town?

Megan asked herself the question the fifth day after Luke left. Devin was in Seattle gathering evidence on a fraud case, and from the sound of his daily calls, Luke was going to be a busy hotel tycoon for some time.

Work.

Work was always the answer.

But in this case, there was a slight problem. She had been working, probably putting in as many hours as Luke was, and had reached the point where a visit to the plantation was imperative. But Luke had not only told her point-blank to keep away from the place, he had taken the keys with him.

Of course, she hadn't agreed. Not verbally. Picking up the phone and poking a few buttons, she wondered if a jury would consider a nod an agreement. Not if they were women, she decided. Women would know the difference between a nod that said "I hear you" and one that was a definite agreement.

"John?" Megan asked when a deep voice answered on the second ring. "This is Megan. I have to go out to the plantation, and Luke took the keys with him when he went out of town. May I stop in and get a duplicate set?" She listened to the rumbling voice, then said, "Doesn't want me to go out there without him? Hmm. I can't imagine what he said that made you think that. Great. In an hour or so? Thanks, I'll be there."

She replaced the receiver and smiled. Realtors were really very nice people. And, of course, John was a cousin.

The afternoon flew by.

Megan went through the house room by room, inch by inch, exactly as she had done before. Touching, absorbing, being welcomed into the past.

She left the kitchen for last, dutifully noting the corner that Luke had chalked off. Dry rot, she vaguely remembered. Or termites. Or both.

She was definitely going to have a talk with Luke, Megan decided, closing her eyes and brushing the wall with her fingertips as she slowly stepped off the outer perimeter of the room.

Come up with a different game plan. Or something.

Knowing he was hovering in the doorway, watching, his dark gaze all over her was . . . distracting. Yeah, that was as good a word as any. *Distracting.* He was definitely that.

She stopped in the far corner, her lips curving in a small, very satisfied smile. Yes, he did sidetrack her, but he did it very well, she reflected. Very well, indeed.

But then, Luke seemed to do everything well—all the way from the casual ease with which he wielded a knife to making a woman cling and demand more.

A slight vibration in the wall caused Megan to flatten her hand and lean closer, her russet brows creased in a frown. Always before, the feelings had been mental rather than physical. Always before . . .

Megan's eyes snapped open and she looked down, noting the chalk marks surrounding her. Stupid, really stupid, she thought as ominous cracking and splintering sounds filled the room. It happened too fast, just as she pushed away from the wall, preparing to leap to safety.

Megan shrieked in pure terror as the floor opened up beneath her.

Several minutes later, flat on her back on a hard-packed dirt floor, staring up at the jagged hole, Megan decided she was going to live. She had the breath knocked out of her and her heart was rattling her ribs, but everything else seemed to be in working order.

First things first, she told herself, taking a shaky breath that contained as much dust as oxygen. Invisible fingers probed her mind, inquiring, anxious, knowing there was a problem, asking if she needed help.

Devin.

They had never figured out how they did it; the ability simply existed. Had always, would always. She reassured him the same way he had inquired. Mentally. She was fine, she responded. Just fine.

"Yeah, I'm terrific," she muttered.

Looking around, she decided she was in the section Luke had pointed out the day they had crawled beneath the house. Possibly a cellar or storage room that had been sealed off. Well, she had apparently found a new entrance. Luke would be thrilled.

"Let's look on the bright side here," she mumbled, getting to her feet. "There aren't any rats." That was about all that could be said for it, she decided. Her prison was small, about five feet by five.

And deep.

She raised up on her toes and stretched as far as she could reach, then settled back with disgust. The beams through which she had fallen still looked sturdy but were at least a good foot above her raised hands.

Unfortunately, the room was also empty. Not a ladder or stool in sight. No cupboard with provisions for unexpected visitors. No water. No bathroom.

It was going to be a long night.

Megan sat on the floor and leaned back against the dirt wall, taking stock. Luke would be back soon, and once he returned, he'd turn the island upside down until he found her. More than likely, he'd start at her house, then probably the plantation. And since her car was outside—although not in the place they usually parked—he'd find it if he looked hard enough. And if he didn't get back, Mr. Kimura's merry men were going to be swarming all over the place in a few days.

So she wouldn't die. She might get a little thirsty, but she'd survive. She pushed aside the ugly thought of dehydration.

"I'll be okay," she said firmly. If worse came to worst, she could send an SOS to Devin. But since they had never perfected the telepathy, he'd still have to come back from Seattle and start looking.

It would be easier to work on Luke, she decided. It was something she had planned to do, anyway, since she had no intention of having a weaker link with her husband than her brother.

It was odd how things worked, she mused, settling into a more comfortable position. If she were more certain about reincarnation, she might believe that Luke and she were later versions of the original builders. The man had been crazy in love with his wife, but unable to say the words. She knew that as surely as she knew that Luke loved her.

Yeah. She grinned. She knew it, but she wasn't going to let him off the hook. Somewhere along the way, the other man had learned, and Luke could, too. Sooner, preferably, than later. Megan had the definite feeling that she wasn't nearly as patient as the other woman had been.

And since he couldn't tell her until he got here, she was damn well going to get him here.

"Okay, Luke darling, let's get this show on the road."

Megan smiled, remembering the one occasion her sister, Liann, had asked how the twin communication worked.

"I don't know exactly," she recalled saying. "Maybe it's a form of meditation. All I know is I clear my mind of everything else and focus on Devin like a laser."

It hadn't been much of an explanation, but that was as good as it got. And that's exactly what she was going to do now.

Focus.

On Lucas McCall.

The hours passed, and Megan found she wasn't too uncomfortable. After all the years she'd spent tuning in to old homes, she was accustomed to the hours spent in quiet. And with her eyes closed, she wasn't aware of being enclosed in darkness once the sun set.

The next morning she opened her eyes and glanced at her watch in the dim light. She sighed, supposing she couldn't expect miracles, and got up to walk around and study the walls again. They didn't look any easier to dig than they had yesterday. Especially since all she had to work with was her fingernails.

No, she'd have better luck calling Luke. Settling back down, she closed her eyes and . . .

Focused.

When she woke up, it was late afternoon. She yawned and raised her arms over her head. Freezing in mid-stretch, she listened, realizing that the sound of footsteps had awakened her. They stopped in the vicinity of the kitchen door, and she heard a savage oath. A moment later, she looked straight up into Luke's face.

His furious face.

His beautiful face.

"Hi." She cleared her throat and tried again. "Hi."

As usual, Luke didn't waste time on preliminaries. "What the *hell* are you doing down there?"

"I fell."

"When?"

"Yesterday afternoon."

"Are you hurt?"

She shook her head. "No."

"Then you're damned lucky," he muttered, checking the beams and what was left of the flooring. "You aren't supposed to be here. I distinctly remember telling you—"

"You came," she interrupted joyfully. "I called you and you came."

"Watch your eyes," he ordered, ripping back some wood to enlarge the hole. "Well, I'd like to say I heard you, but I was in San Francisco, remember?"

"Exactly!" Megan almost purred. "The way I called, you wouldn't have heard if you'd been in the next room."

Luke's eyes narrowed. "Don't even start with the voodoo. I'm not in the mood. I came because . . ."

"Because?"

"There was a perfectly logical reason. You weren't answering your phone." He grunted and pulled back another rotted board. "I rented a car at the airport and came right here."

"Why here?" she asked, retreating to the corner to avoid the worst of the dust and splinters.

"Because I knew you'd be here."

"Ah. You knew. How do you suppose you knew?" She smiled smugly.

"Because you are the most stubborn, reckless and maddening woman in the world. Where else would you be but the one place where you'd be guaranteed to find trouble?" He tested the beams again, resting his weight on them.

When Megan realized what he was doing, she said, "No! Don't come down here. We'll both—"

Luke slid down between the boards and stood towering over her.

"—be trapped." She glared at him, forgetting her satisfaction for the moment. "What an idiotic thing to do! You were supposed to get a ladder or throw me a rope or—"

Luke grabbed her and kissed her until they were both out of breath. When he raised his head, he scowled down at her. "If I did that," he panted, "I'd be too far away to throttle you."

"Is that what you call it?" Megan grinned. "Tell me again why you came here."

His frown grew even blacker. "Megan, don't start with that stuff, okay? I have the psychic ability of a doorknob, so forget it. I came because you're impulsive and don't have a scrap of self-preservation in your whole body. And on top of that—"

She wrapped her arms around his waist and hugged him. "You love me to distraction."

"Of course I love you, you crazy woman," Luke roared, shaking her and sending the dust flying. He touched her face with a shaking hand. "I never thought I'd fall in love. Hell, I didn't even know what love was. I never thought I'd find a woman like you."

Or anyone to love you, she thought, close to tears.

"I love your humor, your stubborn recklessness, your dreams, your softness, your blazing temper. Don't ever doubt that I love you," he said in a tender voice, kissing the tears that were leaving silver tracks in her dirty face. "How many times do I have to say it before you believe it?"

"I know you do," Megan said with a shaky sigh, "but once a day for the rest of our lives would be nice."

He dropped another quick kiss on her mouth, then said, "You got it. Now we'd better get out of here. I want to get some food in you. Then a shower, then bed."

"Terrific idea. I thought of it last night. How?"

"Easy as pie."

And it had been, Megan thought later, watching Luke get out of bed and pad naked across the room. He had lifted her up until she could grasp the beams; then, with his large hand on her bottom, he'd given her another boost that got her up and out. He had followed on her heels, swinging up like a gymnast.

They had taken a shower together, eaten and gone to bed—but not to sleep. They both needed to touch, to love and believe that they had made it through the storm.

Luke had not only shown her, he'd told her that he loved her, over and over again, saying the word like a prayer as he caressed her.

Now he reappeared, hauling in two huge, flat packages, the ones that had been propped by the door when they'd driven up.

"Here, open this one first. It's heavy, so you'd better come over here."

Megan threw back the covers and went to him. "What is it?"

He grinned in anticipation. "Open it."

Megan tore off the paper and helped pull off the protective box. "Oh. Oh, Luke."

She blinked back tears and ran her hand over the beautiful carving. It was a replica of the logo she'd created for Luke. The large Hawaiian figure, with torch uplifted, was painted and lacquered. It looked real enough to step out of the wood.

"It's for the road," he explained with another grin, looking like a naked Santa Claus. "We'll put it right where people turn into the drive. They'll take one look at your work and know they're coming to a very special place."

"Oh, Luke." Megan sat back on her heels and looked up to him, thinking how wrong she'd been. He may not have been able to say the words, but he knew how to love. Right from the start.

"Now this one," he said, propping the carved sign against the wall and placing the other box in front of her. It was just as unwieldy as the first and took a minute or two. When the box was ready to slide off, Luke said, "Close your eyes."

Megan obeyed, resting her hands on her knees. Luke watched her with tender eyes, knowing he would never forget this moment. Naked, with her glorious hair tumbling over her shoulders and breasts, she was all woman.

His woman.

He cleared his throat. "Now."

Megan opened her eyes, and wept. The painting was just as she'd visualized—a large, rambling house looking much like a huge grass shack, but far more substantial, with deep eaves, large windows and a wraparound porch. A dazzling rainbow began at the horizon behind the trees and appeared to end in the center of the roof. At the bottom, an engraved brass plate read Rainbow's End.

Luke put the painting aside and sat beside Megan, pulling her into his arms, wondering at his luck. He was worth a fortune and yet he'd found a woman who wept with joy over something worth a few hundred dollars. A woman who loved him as much as he loved her.

He held her, nuzzling his cheek in her hair, working his fingers down her elegant spine, soothing, just being, letting her know he was there.

Forever.

Giving one last sniff, Megan looked up and gave him a swift kiss. "Now it's my turn." She moved away and brought something out of the closet. It was the chest. "I've been oiling it while you've been gone, and I think it's ready for the grand opening. Of course," she said doubtfully, "there may be nothing in it, but you still get the honors."

It opened easily, and when Luke raised the lid, they both looked in.

"A book," Megan said hopefully, gazing down at a leather-bound volume. "Open it—hurry."

Luke took it out, carefully lifting back the cover. "The journal of Charles McKenzie, Hawaii, June 1890."

"A journal. Omigod, a journal. His journal. Oh, Luke, it's really his—our man." She scooted next to him, almost incoherent with excitement, snuggling against him when he wrapped his arm around her, pulling her closer. They leaned back against the bed, the book propped in Luke's lap.

Megan took a ragged breath as he turned to the first page.

She said yes.
Before the year's end, my sweet Jenny will be my
wife.

The silence of the room was broken only by the sound of turning pages. Long minutes later, they looked up, black eyes meeting blue.

"And they called it Rainbow's End," Luke said quietly.

Megan nodded, wondering what he was thinking. Everything she had told him about the old house and the owners had been verified.

Everything. Right down to the linoleum and making love on the attic floor.

"It's okay, sweetheart. It's okay." Luke's eyes were tender. "I know I have a special lady on my hands, and I'll guard her with my life."

Megan sniffed, too touched to respond, too emotional to answer the ringing telephone. Instead, she let the answering machine pick up the call. She wished she hadn't when she heard her mother's voice.

"Darling, I do think it's time you and Luke visit Uncle Loe. More than time. Uncle Loe thinks so, too. Luke will understand and approve."

Luke looked down at Megan quizzically. "I already said we'd have the blessing. But the opening is a long time away."

"Uh, Luke, there's something I didn't tell you about Uncle Loe."

"Oh, God. What now?"

"His other specialty is wedding ceremonies. He's a minister, and he's married everyone in the family."

Luke, having geared himself for something ominous, gave a shout of laughter and pulled her onto his lap. When he calmed down, he said, "Your mom's right. I do approve. How soon can we get married?"

Megan took a deep breath. "As soon as your parents can get here." When Luke stiffened, she hugged him and said, "Everyone deserves a second chance."

"They've got what they want," he said evenly. "Money."

"And loneliness, Luke. As well as regret."

"How do you know?"

She put his hand to her heart and said softly, "I just know. If it doesn't work out, then at least we've tried. Luke, darling, we have enough love to share. And they're going to be the grandparents of our children. Please."

He sighed. "All right. We'll try. Is there anything else you have to tell me? Anything at all? Like maybe you read crystal balls? Run with werewolves? Anything?"

Megan's lips touched his throat as she smiled. Surely he didn't mean anything as innocent as her telepathy with Devin. Or her certainty that her link with her husband would be even stronger. Or the fact that she really did have what the old people called healing hands. Nah, she assured herself, he couldn't mean things like that.

"Only that I love you with all my heart," she murmured. "Forever."

Luke's arms tightened convulsively around her. "That's all I need. Forever. And that's how long I'll love you, sweetheart. For a lifetime."

She raised her brows. "Even the spooky part of me?"

"Especially the spooky part."

Megan's laugh was like liquid joy. She reminded herself to tell him later about their children. That they would probably inherit the gift. Especially if both parents had it.

*   *   *   *   *

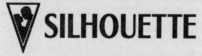

SILHOUETTE

Desire

COMING NEXT MONTH

FAMILY FEUD
Barbara Boswell

Man of the Month

Shelby thought her blue blood couldn't mix with Garrett's blue-collar background. But Garrett vowed that before long he'd be teaching her about mergers and acquisitions…of the most intimate kind!

THE UNFORGIVING BRIDE
Joan Johnston

Children of Hawk's Way

Falcon Whitelaw had vowed never to get married. So why was he saying 'I do' to widowed mother Mara—a woman who hated his guts?

LEMON
Lass Small

Brown Brothers

Lemon Covington hated fortune-hunting females who wanted big rings on their fingers. Then he met Renata—but she wouldn't bother to notice him. So what could this confirmed bachelor do?

SILHOUETTE Desire

COMING NEXT MONTH

MEGAN'S MIRACLE
Karen Leabo

Megan was flabbergasted when Holt Ramsey claimed she was the natural mother of his adopted son! But why was there something hauntingly familiar about the boy?

OUTBACK NIGHTS
Emilie Richards

Russet Ames thought she was on her way to a new life in Australia. But she hadn't counted on old family friend Daniel Marlin meeting her at the airport…

UNDER THE BOARDWALK
Carla Cassidy

Greyson Blakemore was back—and he wouldn't let Nikki forget about the fiery kisses they'd once shared. But Nikki had vowed never to let him back into her life…

COMING NEXT MONTH FROM

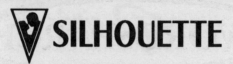 SILHOUETTE

Sensation

*A thrilling mix of passion, adventure
and drama*

SECRET FIRES Kristin James
COLD, COLD HEART Ann Williams
KIDNAPPED! Kate Carlton
WICKED SECRETS Justine Davis

Intrigue

*Danger, deception and desire—
new from Silhouette...*

SQUARING ACCOUNTS Patricia Rosemoor
CUTTING EDGE Caroline Burnes
DÉJÀ VU Laura Pender
CACHE POOR Margaret St. George

Special Edition

Satisfying romances packed with emotion

THE PARSON'S WAITING Sherryl Woods
A HOME FOR THE HUNTER Christine Rimmer
RANCHER'S HEAVEN Robin Elliott
A RIVER TO CROSS Laurie Paige
MIRACLE CHILD Kayla Daniels
FAMILY CONNECTIONS Judith Yates